RISING RIVER

by
LINDEN GRIERSON

CHAPTER ONE

MISS ANNE CARRINGTON-SMITH gazed out of the window across the sunlit sparkling waters of Rose Bay and yawned. Absently she followed the progress of the Manly ferry as it moved with white foam round its bow towards the Heads and turned her attention from that to the flying boat anchored a little way out in the Bay. Tonight it would rise like a cumbersome bird from the water and as it gained height it would also gain grace and speed, then it would head out to sea on the lonely hop to New Zealand. Neither the sight of the ferry nor the flying boat interested her at all, for she had crossed the harbour many times and she had been a passenger on the flying boat on at least three trips. And as she possessed a pilot's licence the thought of flying anywhere did not bring even a flutter to her heart.

Among the medley of boats, yachts and motor cruisers anchored round the wide beautiful sweep of the bay was "The Flying Cloud," one of her numerous possessions. In the garage at the back of the block of flats where she lived was a long, low powerful car. In the room behind her was more tangible evidence of her wealth and her latest whims, and hanging in the spacious built-in cupboards of her lovely bedroom were suits, frocks and evening gowns purchased in London, Paris and New York, with accessories picked up in almost every country in the world.

None of these things pleased her at the moment. For Miss Carrington-Smythe was bored.

Recently life had been a succession of balls, parties, race meetings and charity fêtes, and drifting from one to another with a party of friends she had wondered one day just what was the point in this rather aimless existence. They all went places but rarely seemed to get anywhere, they did things and there was no personal satisfaction upon their completion, they laugh and the laughter sounded high and brittle, they talked and the words were empty and meaningless. Anne had had the feeling there was more to be got from life, and she frowned as she wondered what she was missing and what all her money had failed to buy her.

Her companion, lying full length on a cane day bed, with soft brightly coloured cushions under her head, opened a brightly painted mouth and cried:

"Darling! Who are you scowling at down there?"

"There's something missing somewhere," said Anne softly, sitting with her chin in her cupped hands and staring vacantly across the room.

"I'm bored."

Frowning thoughtfully, her friend Barbara lighted a cigarette and placed it between her lips, waiting to hear more. This wasn't like Anne, although, now she came to think of it, she had been quiet of late and had had little enthusiasm for the many parties they had attended, and once she had actually yawned in the face of her escort at a dance.

"I think I'll go to work," announced Anne, and Barbara sat down abruptly.

"*Work?*" she gasped. "Work? You? Why, you wouldn't know how!"

6

There was a great deal of truth in that, thought Anne grimly. She had never worked in her life. She scowled at the highly polished floor and Barbara studied her anxiously, looking for signs of insanity. But the deep brown eyes held no hint of madness and the wide white forehead was unlined, as was the skin beneath her eyes and round the lovely red mouth. Anne Carrington-Smythe was not one of Sydney's reigning beauties, but she was attractive and instinctively she knew how to dress and bring out her best points to the greatest advantage. She was slim, perhaps too slim for her five foot eight and a half.

"I could learn to work," she said slowly, and her friend became speechless. "Yes, I could learn. There must be dozens of things I could do that would occupy my time and give me the feeling that I was being of some use to the community."

"B-but how would you start?" stammered Barbara, pushing her hand through her hair. "How does one learn these things? Surely you do sufficient for the community when you attend balls in aid of various charities or when you arrange parties in aid of something else. What else is there to do?" She looked puzzled. "I know girls work in shops and cafés, but they haven't the money you have, and there always seem to be plenty dashing about the streets, especially when you're in a hurry. I nearly knocked two over the other day in Market Street –"

Anne stopped her with a movement of impatience. "Barbara, you're nothing but a snob! You can't see any further than the end of your pretty nose. There are other things besides shops and offices. Girls and women enter professions, there are women doctors and lawyers."

"You're too old to start training for that kind of work," retorted Barbara unkindly. "And it takes years before you qualify. Even nurses –"

"I have no desire to be a nurse."

Barbara started to pace the floor. She did not take Anne seriously, this desire to work, or to do something useful for the community was only a passing phase because the other was tired of the round of gaiety. Perhaps she had been overdoing it and needed a holiday.

"Perhaps Roddie could suggest something that would help you scratch somewhere," she said sarcastically at last, and before Anne realised what she was doing Barbara was lifting the phone and dialling a number. She hesitated and sat back. Let her ring Roddie or anyone else, it did not matter. Her mind was made up. She was going to find some work and abandon altogether the life of a society girl. The problem remained though, where was she going to find a job and what could she do? It was all going to be very difficult, for she had no training at all for any job.

"Roddie?" Barbara's voice took on a different tone. "Darling, it's Babs. I'm ringing from Anne's – you must come over immediately! She's ill – no, not quite ill but definitely sickening for something. Oh, no – no spots! But, Roddie," her voice rose higher, "she wants to go out to work! Can you imagine it? Yes, truly. W.O.R.K. I know. it sounds horrid! She's quite serious about it, though. What's that? Oh, Roddie, could you? Bless you, yes, we'll be here."

The phone was replaced on the stand and Barbara surveyed her friend with a hint of laughter in her eyes.

"Roddie says he'll be right over and will bring some of the gang with him."

"Whatever for?" snapped Anne.

"To help me change your mind. He says he's never heard anything so mirthmaking!" She danced back to the window. "It *is* funny, you know, Anne. I can't imagine you working! But if you can find something that's really interesting I might join you for the novelty of it. Fancy *earning* some money!" she had another fit of the giggles at the thought of it and decided to enter into the fun of the moment and so keep Anne occupied until the others arrived. Once they were here they would soon laugh her out of this fit of melancholy. "What could we do? Open a flower shop? Oh, an air hostess! That's what Betty thingummy did. Not that she had any need to, her father has a property somewhere and they have simply oodles of money. She did it for the excitement and then married the pilot."

At the mention of a property Anne's heart had missed a beat. She owned a property somewhere, of that she was quite convinced. It had been left to her years before by her father's brother. Where was it? She frowned thoughtfully, suddenly wishing she had taken more notice of what her solicitor had told her when he reviewed her monetary situation a few months ago. It was quite a large property she believed, somewhere West, in the outback, and that was all she knew of it.

Jumping to her feet, she announced she was going out and Barbara came out of her daydreams with a start.

"But Roddie is on his way here."

"Drat Roddie!"

"And the gang –"

"Drat the gang too," said Anne cheerfully. "Give them lunch, take them on the *Flying Cloud*, do anything you like, but I'm going out."

"Where to?" wailed Barbara.

"To find a job."

Despite the protests and finally the tears, Anne left her flat a few minutes later with a very determined look in her eyes. the low green car was backed out of the garage and slid into the traffic, joining the ever-moving flow into the city. As she began the slow crawl down George Street. She thought again how weary she was of this kind of life. She had a wild longing to go back to Nature, to be among trees and cows instead of cars, trams and high buildings. And what better place than her own property?

Finding a parking space became the most important of her worries for the following half-hour. At last she managed to squeeze her car into a narrow space between a lorry and a luxurious sedan. After locking the doors she had to walk back two blocks to where she wished to go, and being jostled by rushing pedestrians did not improve her temper.

The city appalled her and she turned thankfully into a large building nearby and waited for the lift. Three minutes later she entered a door which led to her solicitor's office and her heart gave an excited little leap. This was the beginning of an adventure.

"Can I help you?" The girl who came towards her was a stranger and Anne drew off her gloves.

"You may tell Mr. Maynard that Miss Carrington-Smythe wants to see him. Immediately," she added, and as she waited she wondered if this slip of a girl ever tired of coming into the office each day and sitting behind a typewriter translating from pages covered with squiggly writing. Most probably she had a boy-friend who would be waiting for her in the evening and together they would ride home in one of their atrocious trams or maybe cross the Harbour on one of the ferries and plan their night out. There would also be a family waiting for her, a father and mother, maybe two or three sisters, and brothers. Her imagination failed her there, for she had no family of her own; her father had died years ago, and her mother – involuntarily a smile crossed her lips when she thought of her mother – was at this moment in Papeete, "Painting the most beautiful pictures of palm trees, pet," she had written in her last letter.

"Mr. Maynard is disengaged and will see you now, Miss Smythe."

Her solicitor was standing by his desk, his lined face looking white in the artificial light, and he held out his hand to greet one of his wealthiest clients.

"This is a surprise," he cried. "A delightful surprise. Sit down, Miss Carrington-Smythe, and do tell me how I can be of service to you."

"Thank you." Anne sat down, crossed one elegant leg over the other as she leaned back in her chair and was amused at the other's glance at her expensive suit and hat. "Mr. Maynard, I want to know all you can tell me of the property I own somewhere."

"Your property?" His eyebrows lifted a little. "Certainly. My partner deals with all this, you know, it's something he had done for you for years, but he's – er – away at present. However, I'll ask Miss Roberts to bring in the files."

They waited in silence until Miss Roberts returned with a thick file which she placed before the solicitor and withdrew silently. He cleaned his spectacles and cleared his throat as he turned over page after page.

"Let me see now. It was left to you by your Uncle Claud, your father's brother, that is. He died four years ago. Everything is here and in perfect order, Miss Carrington-Smythe. Financially it was a very sound proposition and the money received from the estate was to be kept in trust until you became of age. You were twenty-one three years ago, were you not? Since then you have been – er – enjoying your uncle's legacy." He glanced at her again. Mr. Maynard did not quite approve of the manner in which Miss Carrington-Smythe had been enjoying the proceeds from the estate, but it was not his place to say so. "It seems to me," he said thoughtfully, glancing at the papers again, "that the property has not been as bountiful of late, despite the high prices prevailing for both wool and wheat. I should study this at greater length, as I told you before my partner deals with this and I am – er – rather unfamiliar with the whole. However, the income seems to have dropped steadily. I can't understand it, but no doubt there is a reason for it."

Anne nodded. "Who is in charge there, Mr. Maynard?"

"The manager's name is Norton, John Norton. He was with your uncle for fifteen years, maybe more, and was quite reliable. Although, without wishing to be uncharitable, Miss Carrington-Smythe, from the looks of things, he does not seem to have been pulling his weight of recent times. And also, without wishing to be too – er – personal, there has been no interest shown by you as the – er – owner, during the past four years. Without the personal touch, shall I say, things are bound to get slack."

"I realise that." Anne bit her lip and watched him as he thumbed through the papers. "What is the name of the property?"

"Gum Valley. And its position is – er – about three hundred miles from Sydney. On the Macquarie River. Definitely out West," he added.

Anne's fingers started to beat a rapid tattoo on the arms of her chair. She had never been inland before, there was nothing to interest the gang away from the cities and the coast, although she had flown over the country many times and from what she could recollect of those flights was monotonous miles of tree-covered country, with long wide stretches of plains, where she presumed, they grew the wheat and tended the sheep. Suddenly she felt wholly ignorant of what went on in this great continent.

Mr. Maynard made a quick movement.

"Ah!" he exclaimed, as though he had made a great discovery. "I knew something had passed through my hands just recently regarding Gum Valley. With Mr. Jeen being away it naturally came to my attention." He turned to a pile of letters in a tray on his desk and glanced through them swiftly, extracting one near the bottom of the pile. "This is it. Oh, dear, it's nothing important, I'm afraid. I thought it was. This letter arrived at the beginning of the week, asking, among other things, for an advertisement to be inserted in the papers for the services of a cook. Asking is not the word, now I come to read it through again. *Demanding* the services of a cook."

"And have the services of a cook been obtained?" she asked quickly.

Regretfully the solicitor shook his head. "I fear not. One or two did reply to the advertisement, I interviewed them here, but – er – as soon as I mentioned the distance from the nearest township, they – er – cried off, as the saying goes."

Anne leaned forward. "What is the distance from the nearest township, Mr. Maynard?"

"Approximately thirty-two miles." He leaned back and folded his hands over his lean stomach, peering at her through his spectacles with kindly interest. "I believe that is one of the principal reasons why people these days will not – er – go to work in the country. They are so far from the towns, there are no shops, no cinemas, in fact few of what are called the amusements. It's a lonely life out there in the bush, Miss Carrington-Smythe."

"It sounds like Paradise," she breathed, and in his surprise he all but lost his spectacles as he sat upright.

"Paradise?" he repeated.

"Yes. Just imagine! No dressing up, no photographers, no heart-burnings because your best friend is wearing a more expensive gown! No rush and bustle, no noise – nothing! I would call it going back to Nature with a vengeance."

"So would I," he remarked dryly.

Miss Anne Carrington-Smythe began to smooth the fingers of her expensive Italian gloves and he waited, wondering what was passing through her mind. Drawing up her chair nearer to the desk, she demanded to be told all about Gum Valley and the exact state of its finances, and for the next twenty minutes she listened to his precise voice reeling off figures and numbers until her head buzzed. Mr. Maynard seemed puzzled at the state of affairs on the property, there was no doubt that things had gone rapidly downhill since the death of Claud Carrington-Smythe, especially during the past eighteen months.

Finally Anne leaned back satisfied and she looked very much in earnest as she said, "Write or wire to the property and say you've engaged a cook for six months –"

"But I haven't, dear Miss Carring –"

"Oh, yes, you have. I'm the new cook."

His jaw dropped. "You! You're not in earnest, you can't be!"

"I am and I can. Look, two hours ago I was telling my friend that I was heartily sick of the round of parties, races, fêtes and what-nots which have been my lot recently. I'm bored, Mr. Maynard, bored and tired, and my nerves are going to pieces." She glanced at him appealingly and he was quite prepared to believe that her nerves were not all they should be when she looked at him in that manner. "I've been wondering what I could do and the thought of Gum Valley sounded just the answer to all my problems, but I've been wondering, while you've been talking, how I could go there and be just an ordinary person – a girl without a fortune. Going as the cook is the complete answer. It's a marvellous idea. I'll earn my own living and no one will know who I am."

"But *can* you cook?" he asked.

"As well as most girls, I think," she replied, thinking of the fancy concoctions she made when the gang descended upon her unexpectedly and demanded a meal.

"But cooking outback is not the same as – er – cooking in the city, Miss Carrington-Smythe," he said with reproof in his voice as he recovered himself somewhat. "You'll be cooking for a number of hungry men –"

"How many men will there be?" she interrupted to ask.

"Let me see." He began to treat this as a piece of frivolity on her part, for try as he could, he could not imagine Anne Carrington-Smythe in the role of cook at Gum Valley, which was a very outlandish place from what he could make out. "There's John Norton, the manager, I've mentioned him. A very reliable man. Or he was. Then there's the man who's been signing these letters of late, very abrupt letters, too. Kennedy, yes, that's his name. There is also a groom and a gardener." He turned to another page of figures. "Wages are also paid to three other men. That makes seven in all."

"I'm going," she stated definitely. "How do I get there?"

The solicitor blinked. "You aren't going *now*?"

"As soon as I can."

"Before you change your mind?"

"No! I'm going because I want to go and for that reason only. Do you think I would enter into a thing like this light-heartedly, without any thought on the subject?" she asked indignantly. "I'm not that kind of a person!"

"Candidly, Miss Carrington-Smythe, I don't know what kind of person you really are!" he cried with severity. "You haven't had the time to give this much thought at all. I think you'd best go home and sleep on the idea, it will probably seem different tomorrow."

Anne thrust out her jaw. She could be very stubborn at times. "I'm going! I'll make a success of it too, you see!" She scribbled rapidly on a sheet of paper. "There! send this wire to Mr. Kennedy. 'Have hired cook on six months' contract. She'll be leaving Sydney on –' hum, let me see!" Thoughtfully she bit on the end of the pencil. "Ring up the station, please, there's a dear, and enquire about trains. I don't even know which line it's on."

"It's on the way to Bourke."

"Bourke? Why, that's the back of beyond!" she exclaimed.

"So is Gum Valley," cried Mr. Maynard, glancing furtively at his watch. She caught his glance and looked down at her own wrist.

"It's lunchtime."

"Past lunchtime," he agreed with asperity. Wealthy young ladies who suddenly developed ideas about becoming cooks did not warrant a great deal of fuss making of them.

"I'm sorry," Anne apologised, smiling at him brilliantly. "Look, you come and have lunch with me, then we can discuss this further and I'll finish the telegram to send to the abrupt Mr. Kennedy."

With a sigh he reached for his hat and together they left the deserted office and closed the door.

CHAPTER TWO

MR. MAYNARD was to remember that lunch for a long time to come. Anne made her plans with great rapidity and also made Mr. Maynard promise that under no circumstances would he divulge her whereabouts to any inquisitive friends.

"For if you do," she explained, "they'll all immediately drive out there for the sole purpose of watching me work. During the time I'm there I'll live solely on what I earn." She paused thoughtfully. "I suppose I can live on a cook's wages?"

"Thousands of others do," he replied, and she flashed him a glance of annoyance.

"Need you put a damper on everything, Mr. Maynard? Must you look as if I've announced that I'm contemplating a life of crime instead of earning my living for once?"

He thought that maybe it was a crime to entrust the welfare of seven hard-working men to the slim hands of this young lady.

"If you go," there was still some doubt in his mind about the outcome of this impulsiveness, "you'll be able to investigate affairs out there and find out why Gum Valley has ceased to pay those rich dividends and why the revenue has dropped since your uncle's death."

"Yes, I shall do that," she agreed absently. "As to the trains," she went on, "I wonder if this hotel happens to have a railway guide? I could study it while we have coffee."

The railway guide revealed three trains a week to Bourke, leaving Sydney on Sunday, Tuesday and Thursday evenings and arriving at Murra Creek, the nearest station to Gum Valley, about eleven o'clock the following morning. At that information Anne's face paled; she was a poor train traveller, much preferring to travel by car, plane or ship.

The outcome of that was that she decided to go most of the way by car. The thought of spending a whole night propped in one corner of a compartment with no privacy at all appalled her, and the journey would be completed by train. The telegram was completed and dispatched, and after telling Mr. Maynard that in future she was to be known only as Anne Smith and that all letters had to be addressed to her by that name, she said goodbye and returned to her flat to begin preparations for her departure.

There was no one there to meet her, for which she was thankful. Barbara, Roddie and the gang had evidently become tired of waiting and had departed in search of other pleasures. But the following afternoon when she was busy putting away some of her most priceless treasures, the doorbell rang and going into the hall she was met by a solitary young man, who smiled at her cheerfully.

"Our busy little bee!" he exclaimed. "I've come to see if what Barbara told me yesterday was true."

"Come in, Roddie." She led the way into the lounge and he followed her slowly.

Roderick Hall was a good-looking young man with a clipped military moustache and dark, devil-may-care eyes. He drove a wicked-looking car and caused backward glances no matter where he went. He was extremely popular with his friends and Anne had always got along very well with him; the announcement of their engagement had been long awaited by the other members of the gang.

Roddie glanced at the room, bare of many of its treasures, and raised his eyebrows.

"So it was true?" he asked.

"Yes," answered Anne quietly. "I'm going to work."

He looked at her for a long moment, his eyebrows still raised above his dark eyes.

"Why?"

"Because I'm tired, bored and fed up with my present existence."

"That include your friends too?"

"Yes," she admitted, and he laughed.

"You were always truthful, Anne. Where are you going? Have you really got a job?"

She nodded. "But I have no intention of telling where it is or what it is."

"All right." That was one thing she had always liked about Roddie, he never argued about anything. "But Barbara told me you had the feeling you wanted to do more for the community, that you wanted," his lips twitched slightly, "to scratch beneath the surface to find something worth while. May I make a suggestion, my sweet Anne?"

"Well?" she asked. "What is your suggestion?"

"Only this," he said casually. "That you marry me and stay here. In doing that you would be of some use to the community. I mean, you would be looking after a home and maybe a family—"

"Roddie!" Anne stared at him. He looked serious enough despite the light tone of his voice. "You can't mean it!"

"I do. It's an idea I've had buzzing round for quite a while, rather a nice idea too. But until I realised you were serious about this idea of your own I kept putting off asking you because we seemed to drift along quite happily."

She turned to the windows, surprised and touched. The idea of marrying him had crossed her mind on more than one occasion, but had been lightly dismissed from her thoughts. Roddie was a good friend and she liked him; he must more than like her, she reflected, when he thought of a home life and the possibility of a family. She tried to imagine this young man-about-town in the role of a father and failed completely.

"Well?" he asked softly behind her.

"I'm sorry. My dear, I'm really sorry. You are a dear and I like you, but not sufficiently to marry you –"

"Can't I make you change your mind about this fool idea, Anne? It doesn't sound like you at all, wanting to bury yourself in obscurity. Marry me and we'll have all the fun in the world. We'll go anywhere you want –"

"That's partly the trouble," she cried, turning to face him. "I've been everywhere I want to go and see everything there is to be seen. That's why I'm so tired, I've too much money and seem to have spent my life doing absolutely nothing!"

"Give your money away and come and do something in my house," he suggested promptly, and she smiled.

For a long time they looked at each other. He was very much in earnest and Anne knew it. Gently she put her hand on his arm.

"No, Roddie. I'm sorry," she said again very quietly and definitely.

He sighed. "Are you going to this job for any length of time?"

"Six months at least."

He whistled softly. "May I ask you again when you return home?"

There was no harm in giving him a promise like that, she thought quickly, perhaps after six months at Gum Valley she would be only too thankful to return to Roddie and all that marrying him would mean.

"Yes, you may ask me again when I return," she promised, and with that he was content.

The telephone rang shrilly and she picked up the receiver. It was Mr. Maynard to say he had received an answer to the telegram they had despatched after so much thought.

"It's not very – er – complimentary," he said flatly. "And is signed by that man Kennedy. It says 'Cancel contract for female cook. Not wanted. Male only. Kennedy'!"

Her face flushed a deep scarlet. "How dare he! Female indeed!" She glanced at Roddie who was watching her intently. "Wire again, Mr. Maynard, and inform *Mr*. Kennedy that everything stands as before. Do you understand?"

"Yes, Miss Carrington-Smythe."

The receiver was put down with a bang. When she arrived at Gum Valley she would give that man Kennedy something to think about – then she realised that in the position of cook she could do no such thing.

"Bad news?" asked Roddie solicitously, and her flush deepened.

"No."

"Has Mr. Maynard something to do with your departure into the unknown?" he asked shrewdly.

Anne thought rapidly. Roddie she could trust, but perhaps it would be safer not to say anything to him.

"Naturally he'll be looking after my interests during my absence," she replied, and he nodded.

"Naturally," he agreed with a grin.

He stayed to help with the packing, and after his departure, when he had stopped in the doorway and taken her into his arms, kissing her swiftly and resourcefully, Anne sat down at her writing bureau and wrote a long letter to her mother in

Papeete. Nothing, she knew, would surprise that good lady. The idea of her elegant daughter becoming a cook on a station out West would amuse her immensely, so Anne explained everything in detail, even to describing her feelings about the unknown and insolent Mr. Kennedy. Already she disliked him; never before had she been so rudely and abruptly addressed as a female. That rankled and her indignation spilled itself on to her letter. But as she read it through she smiled to herself; it was silly to take such a dislike to a person she had never met.

The following morning was spent shopping and Anne emerged from one of the large stores in Pitt Street with her arms full of parcels, which contained everything she thought Miss Smith, the cook, would wear. Even in the cheap cotton frocks she looked smart; she was the type of woman who was chic no matter what covered her slim body.

She had a last interview with Mr. Maynard, listened to his carefully phrased homily and requested him to let her flat for the next six months. If she had no home she would not be in too much of a hurry to return. He patted her shoulder with fatherly interest when he said goodbye and watched her go as she left the office, wondering how long it would be before he saw her in there again. If he had been a betting man he would have said she would be back in Sydney within two months, certainly before Christmas, for it would not take her long to discover Gum Valley was not a place for an attractive young lady. He frowned and drew towards him the file relating to the property. He was very puzzled over affairs out there. Once everything had worked smoothly, John Norton had written regularly and they had carried on as they had always done under the guidance of the old man. Mr. Maynard knew there would naturally be a difference as year after year went past and no one ever visited the place, but surely that would not account for the thousands of pounds' difference in the turn-over, knowing, as he did, the high prices which had been received for wheat and wool. Personally he did not like the way the man Kennedy seemed to have taken over the ordering and the supervision. All the letters received from Gum Valley recently had been signed by him and they were very abrupt in tone. Norton was still there, he was drawing his wages every month, but something, somewhere, was not right. A great pity, he thought, that his partner, Mr. Jeen, should happen to be on vacation at this particular time; he knew everything of the working of the estate. Perhaps Miss Carrington-Smythe would find out where the discrepancies were occurring, then he would take appropriate action.

Anne left the city early the following day and joined another stream of traffic on the Parramatta Road.

The way was long, the roads lonely, and each mile took her further from the life she had always known and now wanted to leave, and nearer to the new.

To pass the time as she flashed along the road, she tried to visualize Gum Valley, but the gentle undulating country through which she was passing, with its soft green and sudden vistas of the wide deep valleys, gave her no indication that it would gradually level out into huge expanses of flat, sun-drenched plains, with not a hill to be seen for hundreds of miles.

She was an Australian and had a feeling of shame that she knew so little of the land of her birth or the history of the places through which she passed on the delightful drive to Bathurst a hundred and twenty miles from Sydney.

It was in Bathurst she had her first glimpse of the Macquarie River and she stopped to look at it, hoping it moved as placidly between tree-lined banks out at Gum Valley. This river meandered for many, many miles, heading inland away from the sea, until in time it joined the Darling, that wide river with tributaries extending well into Queensland, and in turn it moved west to join the Murray which met the sea away in South Australia. She shook her head as she thought of it.

The road headed towards the sunset and the bright light

dazzled her eyes. Because she had stopped so long and so often she had not made very good time and was thankful she had allowed herself the extra two days. It would never do for Miss Smith not to arrive on the Bourke Mail on the day she had specified so emphatically on her telegram.

So she slept that night in Orange and had time the following morning to look round the cherry orchards and the huge bulk of Mount Canobolas in the distance. In winter this was often covered in snow and icy blasts blew across the surrounding countryside. Taking to the road again she discovered the hills were more spaced out and more gentle, the land was beginning to level out and paddocks of wheat became more frequent on either hand. After morning coffee in Wellington, she drove the thirty-one miles to Dubbo, her destination, before lunch.

The disposal of the car became her next consideration. Somehow she felt she did not wish to part with it. Together they had driven many thousands of miles and it was the one of her possessions she liked the best. In the end she arranged to leave it indefinitely at one of the garages, thinking as she lifted out her one and only suitcase that she would always have a way of escape, and moved slowly into the main street. The last string had been cut with her former life, she was no longer Miss Carrington-Smythe, she was little Miss Smith, the cook, with no home, no car, nothing beyond this fibre suitcase which held all she possessed.

Anne was on the station early the following morning. The train was already in and half the passengers were having breakfast in the refreshment room. She walked along the platform looking at everything with interest. One carriage was labelled "Through to Brewarrina" and she wondered where on earth Brewarrina was and how long it took to get there.

Another hour would see her at Murra Creek and she began to speculate upon her arrival there, who would meet her and how would she be able to recognise him.

The land levelled out and open paddocks replaced the bush and scrub, paddocks lush with wheat which looked heavy in the sunshine. Soon harvesting would start and heavy tractors and headers would gather in the golden harvest. This is what I shall have to learn about, she thought, the wheat and the wool, and while I'm learning and finding out why Gum Valley is not as prosperous as it used to be, I must cook for seven hungry men.

The train stopped once or twice at lonely sidings and halts, waited a few minutes by the platform of another small town and continued its journey again. Houses began to make their appearance on either side of the line, very scattered houses, each looking drowsy in the clear sunlight, sheltered by trees in their own plots of ground. More white silos stood gaunt and bare in the sidings, an engine was standing stationary with cattle trucks behind it and as they passed Anne had a glimpse of animals and pitied them their journey, then came the beginning of the platform, the name of the station "Murra Creek", then that too was gone and the train stopped with a slight jerk.

Standing on the platform, gripping her case tightly, she looked around. By the exit was a group of men, any one of which could be waiting for her. There was a short man, his rotund middle almost cut in half by the belt he wore, privately she thought he would have done far better to have worn braces. There were two men who looked conspicuous because they were wearing collars and ties, a tall man who was very sunburnt, a man wearing a leather apron over a pair of shorts, and the ticket collector.

She waited uncertainly as people filed slowly past the latter and into the waiting-room beyond, and finally into the dusty station yard. No one claimed her and when the train pulled out she was alone on the platform excepting for packages and parcels, a crate of hens, a few boxes of day-old chicks and three rolls of linoleum.

The ticket collector glanced in her direction.

"Waiting for someone?" he asked cheerily.

Anne moved towards him. "I was to be met," she faltered. "I'm going out to a place called Gum Valley –"

"Oh!" he glanced over his shoulder. "Pat! Lady here wants you, mate!"

The tall man who was very sunburnt turned in his tracks and came back up the steps into the waiting room. The other man indicated the waiting girl with his thumb and after taking her ticket ambled away. Anne was conscious of two cold eyes surveying her from head to toe.

"Are *you* Miss Smith?" he asked slowly, and she nodded.

"Yes, the new cook."

He drew in his breath sharply. "And I told that old fool of a solicitor we didn't want a female," he exploded. "Then he sends me one like you!"

What an excellent beginning, thought Anne angrily, staring at him in turn. This could only be the insolent Mr. Kennedy, no one else would greet her in such a manner, and wild ideas of what she would say to him when she did disclose her identity began to form in her mind in those few moments. That was twice he had referred to her as a female.

Biting her lip, she kept back a scathing retort. Let him do the talking just now; her turn would certainly come one of these days!

"What's wrong with me?" she asked meekly, keeping her voice steady with a great effort.

"You're too young. You'll be too much of a responsibility," he exclaimed. "I think, Miss Smith, you'll be well advised to wait here in town and return to Sydney on the Mail tomorrow night."

"I shall do no such thing!" retorted Miss Smith. "I've been engaged as cook at Gum Valley and as cook I'm going to go!"

It was his turn to bite his lip. "You'll regret it," he said at last.

"Do you think so?"

"I'm sure of it," he answered a trifle grimly. "You're determined to go out here?" Anne nodded her head vigorously and he shrugged his shoulders. "In which case I suppose we shall have to put up with you." He turned away, but not before Anne caught the words which followed and the colour ran high in her cheeks. "You're a confounded nuisance. Gum Valley is no place for a woman."

As he strode ahead into the sunshine she followed him slowly, pondering over his words. Why was Gum Valley no place for a woman? What was going on out there on her property?

A grey utility was parked in the shade of a huge pepper tree, already laden with what looked to be stores; there were cardboard boxes with tins sticking out of the tops, sacks of potatoes and two or three small pieces of machinery. Stopping beside it, he held out his hand for her case.

"I'm Pat Kennedy," he announced. "Get in and when I've collected a few more things we'll make tracks." The tone of his voice was very abrupt and he slammed the door hard as he took his seat and waited, staring straight ahead, until she was settled.

The utility rattled away from the township, and after the comfort and speed of her own car. This felt to have no springs anywhere and it thumped heavily when they turned on to a road which had been worn, by time, wind and erosion, into a series of corrugations. Looking ahead, Anne reflected that it reminded her of a piece of corrugated paper, then her inside claimed her attention. It was moving up and down but not in keeping with the bouncing seat, and with a gasp she turned the lever by her side and let down the window. The speed of the truck moved a cool breeze against her brow and the upheaval within began to subside.

"Are you the manager?" she asked at last innocently.

"No," he frowned. "Officially I'm the jackaroo, but there are times at this joint when I don't know what I am!"

Anne decided it would be in order to show some interest in her destination. Any woman, cook or not, would naturally wish to know something of the place where she was going to live. Probably she would be snubbed for her pains, but that she would have to risk.

"Is it a nice place, this Gum Valley?"

He grinned faintly. "It depends on what you call nice, Miss Smith. I don't think you'll like it." The way he said it suggested that he hoped she wouldn't.

"Indeed? That remains to be seen, Mr. Kennedy."

He shrugged his shoulders, an irritating habit, thought Anne crossly, staring out of her window again. The countryside was appallingly flat, not a mould of earth or ridge of trees broke the long monotony which stretched far away into the distance. There were clumps of oddly twisted gums and paddocks of grey ring-barked trees, stretching pathetically bare branches towards the emptiness of the sky. In those paddocks there must have been hundreds, perhaps thousands of trees, all dead and useless.

"Is nothing done with that wood?" she enquired, waving towards the forest of grey trunks they were passing.

"It's burnt."

"Isn't it of any use for making things?"

"No."

"Why not?"

"Not suitable."

She gave a sigh of exasperation, hoping the other six men at Gum Valley were more talkative than this one.

"How many people are there out here?" she put the question without turning her head.

"Seven."

"Including yourself?"

He nodded. "There's John Norton, the manager. Rusty the groom, Jan, so called because he's a Pole and has a name which ends with 'ski' and no one can pronounce it, Alan, Peter, Dick and me."

"And is it a very big place?" She wanted to know something about it – after all, it was hers.

"Not too big." Which was a very non-committal answer.

"Hang on!" he cried suddenly as they approached a wooden bridge at speed, and she had just time to grab the door handle with one hand and the seat with the other before the utility hit the protruding plank in the decking of the bridge with a terrific thump. Anne half-rose in the seat and fell back with a jar that seemed to wrench her spine.

"I'd forgotten that," he remarked coolly.

With the bump Anne's suitcase, which contained all her possessions, fell on to the bridge, rocked for a moment or two on its end and then fell down into the bed of the creek, fifteen feet below, unnoticed by either of them.

The track wound its way towards a green belt of trees which Anne guessed correctly bordered the river. It was easy to follow the winding course of the river bank, at one moment it was near at hand, then it moved into the distance and twisted back again. There was a glimpse of a red roof through the green of the trees, some outbuilding appeared and the utility came to an abrupt stop beside a thick green hedge. She had arrived at Gum Valley.

Curious faces appeared at doors and windows, someone whistled and her cheeks reddened. This was going to take some getting used to. Rather shyly, holding tightly on to her handbag, she stepped down on to the ground and looked round with great attention.

The outbuildings, the men's quarters obviously, for washing was hanging on the verandah rails, were all shaded by the thick light green of the pepper trees and behind those were sheds and small wheat silos. Behind the hedge were the gardens of the homestead, they looked cool and inviting with shrubs and trees forming large patches of shadow on the green of the grass. Roses were in bloom by the hundred and their perfume drifted towards her on the still air. There was a great peacefulness about the place which appealed to Anne. She could catch a gleam of water away over the first paddocks and hear the gentle lowing of the cattle. Horses were standing beneath the scattered shade of the trees and dogs rummaged round sniffing, brown cattle dogs, slinky and shifty-looking with their yellow eyes. She smiled as she turned to the man at her side.

"It's very pretty. Will you show me round later?"

"If I have time," he replied ungraciously, watching a man come from one of the sheds.

"Who is this?"

"This is Mr. Norton, the manager."

There was a dreamy childlike smile on the face of the new-comer and Anne's heart warmed to him. He looked delicate and almost saintly with his thick crop of white hair which had a faint wave, his eyes were very blue and very trusting, and his hands, she noticed quickly, were white and blue-veined, un-stained by work.

"You've been away a long time, Pat," he said quietly. "Who is this?"

"John, meet Miss Smith, our new cook."

"Miss Smith? I'm delighted, truly delighted to know you," he held out his hand and gave hers a brief shake. "You should have told me you were coming. Pat, why didn't you tell me we were having Miss Smith to live with us?"

"I did tell you. Dozens of times."

"You did?" a faint frown creased his forehead and Anne was silent, sensing something she did not quite understand. Then his face cleared.

"Oh, I remember! This is the Miss Smith you were playing

hell about, isn't it? That's right," he nodded and smiled at the girl. "He said we didn't want you here because you'd be of no use and that in any case you would be a cross-eyed spinster between fifteen and fifty. I remember."

"I'm glad he gave himself such a wide margin," said Anne coldly as a flush mounted her cheeks and she turned to look indignantly at Pat Kennedy. There was a faint smile of amusement round his mouth and he did not look at all put out by the other's blunt disclosure.

"I told Mr. Maynard we didn't want a female cook at Gum Valley," he said, as though some explanation was necessary.

"Fetch my case," she commanded, sounding very like Miss Carrington-Smythe. "Then show me my room."

Pat Kennedy gave her a sidelong glance and moved to the back of the utility, lifting things down on to the ground. She waited impatiently, her lips pressed tightly together, and Mr. Norton waited with her, rocking on his heels, whistling softly under his breath.

"It's not here," announced a voice, and she ran to where Pat Kennedy was standing, his hat on the back of his head as he surveyed the pile of boxes before him.

"Of course it's there! It must be." Her voice trembled a little. "I saw you put it there."

"I'm sorry," he indicated the stores at his feet. "It isn't there now. It must have fallen off somewhere on the road –"

"Oh!" Speechlessly Anne looked at him. "You must find it. Go back along the track until you do!"

"I'll do no such thing," he retorted. "I have plenty to do with my time without chasing back into town looking for your suitcase –"

"B-but I have nothing else," she spread out her hands pathetically. "My clothes – my nightwear." She knew there was nothing out here which could replace that.

"You can't do without nightwear," agreed Mr. Norton. "Pat,

Miss Smith has lost her case and we must do something. Definitely."

"But what? I've already wasted half a day going in there to meet her."

"Can't you send someone else if you're so busy?" pleaded Anne. "I'm sure if you asked one of the other men they would be *delighted* to go and look for it for me."

"Maybe. But it happens that their lunch-hour is now finished and they're to return to ploughing firebreaks. Those, Miss Smith, are of far more importance than your suitcase," said Pat Kennedy curtly. "All I can do is to ring through to town. I met two other chaps in there this morning who come along that road and I'll leave a message asking them to look for it and to drop it in here if they find it. The mail man comes out tomorrow, too, I'll mention it to him. Your name will be on the case?"

"There's a label," she said dully. "But what am I going to do in the meantime?"

"Perhaps we shall find something in the house." He turned away and she followed him slowly.

The room he had prepared for her was clean but very bare. There was a single bed, a small dressing table, a tiny wardrobe behind the door and a chair. A pile of clean linen was on the end of the bed and he waved his hands towards it as he stood in the doorway.

"I left the bed as I'm not much of a hand at making them. There are clean towels in the top drawer of the dressing table and the bathroom is at the end of the passage. Now I'll take you to the kitchen."

He opened another door and stood back. Anne went in slowly. This was to be her domain, here she would spend many hours preparing meals for this man and six others. It was a fairly large room with two windows; it was light but warm. Large tins stood by one wall and she peeped inside. One held sugar, another flour and a smaller one held salt. There was a refrigerator, operated by kerosene, which kept the meat and milk fresh, and for that alone she was thankful.

"You can manage in here?" It was half a question, half a statement.

"Of course!" she answered with great spirit. "It's dirty, although that's only to be expected when there've only been men in here! There are ants all over the place and already I've seen signs of mice –"

"There's rats as well," he offered, leaning against the door-post. "And at night two or three 'possums come in to have a look round."

"Would you please go and make as many enquiries as you can about my case?" she asked icily. "You said there was a phone?"

He nodded as he straightened himself. "But it doesn't always work," he remarked as he left the room.

Anne clenched her hands. Mr. Kennedy seemed intent on putting as many obstacles as he could in her way, but she was not going to be driven away from Gum Valley by him or by anyone else. Obviously it was time someone came to look into affairs here, there was a mystery of some description about the place. But that could wait, what was most important at the moment was a cup of tea and something to eat.

There was plenty of bread, butter, eggs and jam, and on the stove a large urn filled with water was bubbling happily to itself. As she cut bread and buttered it, she realised how quiet it was. The men had returned to work, in the distance she could hear a tractor, there were the soft cluckings from the hens outside and the cries of the birds. Nothing would disturb her here, there would be no blaring motor horns, no clatter of trams or the drone of planes, no shrill voices over the telephone, and she gave a happy little sigh as she poured out the tea and sat down at the table.

But there was still Pat Kennedy. He returned to the kitchen five minutes later.

"The phone was working," he announced. "I left the message and whoever finds your case will bring it along. May I have some tea and something to eat, too?"

She had forgotten he had not eaten and hastened to place other things on the table for him. "What time do you all have a meal tonight?"

"About six. Although today you needn't bother to cook, we decided we'd let you get your bearings first and Jan baked a roast this morning. Breakfast, by the way, is at seven."

"What?" she asked weakly.

"Seven a.m. prompt. We start work at seven-thirty."

"Oh!" Usually at seven a.m. Miss Carrington-Smythe was fast asleep between cool sheets. This meant getting up at the unheard of hour of six, if not before. "And other meals?"

"We have a break at nine-fifteen for smoke-oh, dinner at twelve, smoke-oh again at three-fifteen and another meal at six."

"No supper?" asked Anne wonderingly.

Pat shook his head. "No supper."

They ate in silence for a while, each busy with their own thoughts.

"Where did you get the bed linen from for my room?" she asked suddenly. "It looked exceptionally clean."

"From the house." Pat spread jam liberally over a thick piece of bread. "It's been there for years and as the woman who owns this place can't be bothered to take an interest in it we aren't harming her by borrowing a few sheets and towels. She doesn't even know it's there."

"Do you borrow her things too?"

"What I do in the house is no concern of yours, Miss Smith. But to satisfy your curiosity, I use my own."

"Who *is* the owner of Gum Valley?"

"Some dame in Sydney," he replied, withdrawing an ancient pipe from a pocket. "With so much money to throw about that the income from a property such as this is a mere drop in the ocean." He sounded a trifle bitter and she leaned over the table, her chin in her hands, to gaze at him innocently.

"Have you ever met her?"

"No, thank God! If Miss Carrington-Smythe, that's her name, believe it or not, ever came here she'd soon go away with a flea in her ear!"

"Indeed!" her eyes flashed angrily, "And would you be putting the flea in her ear for her, Mr. Kennedy?"

"Too right! By the time I'd finished with Miss A.C.S. she'd wish herself a thousand miles away!"

Anne bit her lip. "What does the A. stand for?"

"Ada, Annie – I don't know," he said impatiently, standing up, and her five foot eight and a half was insignificant compared with his height. "I suppose I had better show you round, for tomorrow you will be busy and I can't spare any more time, I've wasted enough today as it is."

CHAPTER THREE

At six o'clock Anne met the rest of the men. Mr. Norton was sitting at the head of the table when she went into the dining-room, he raised his head, smiled at her vaguely and promptly forgot her, so it was Pat Kennedy who had to introduce her to the others. Alan the gardener proved to be an old man; he had a permanent stoop and his handshake was soft and flabby. He peered at the girl suspiciously, mumbled something and sat down. Rusty evidently got his name from the colour of his hair, and during the whole time Anne was at Gum Valley she never heard his proper name. He eyed her smilingly and the pressure of his fingers made her raise her head.

"It's going to be quite pleasant having you here with us, Miss Smith," he murmured, and she felt a little shiver run down her spine.

Jan, the Pole, also smiled, but in a different way. He was another big man with a thatch of black hair. Anne guessed his age at about forty and as she shook hands and he spoke to her in excellent English she liked him immediately. Peter was a typical man of the outback, thick-set, brown-faced and very silent. Dick proved to be seventeen, a youngster with bright eyes and a small red mouth in a babyish-looking face, and Anne wanted to mother him.

After she had been introduced she took her seat between Dick and Pat Kennedy and silently began her meal. The men, too, were silent at first, this was the first time a woman had sat at the table with them in their own quarters, then Rusty, who was the most forward of them all, enquired about life in Sydney and the ice was broken. Anne found her tongue again and in response to a question as to why she had come so far out West, confessed the truth, saying she wanted peace and quiet and that she was thankful to leave the city. They immediately looked at her incredulously and she was conscious the whole time of the man sitting by her side, silent but observant, listening to all she had to say with rather a sardonic look on his face.

"Peace and quiet, did you say?" asked young Dick, raising his eyebrows. "The country is never quiet! Always there are the sounds of the birds and the animals, the tractors and the jeep. And us, of course. We aren't exactly a quiet crowd!"

There was a general laugh at that remark and Anne caught the look of warning Pat flung at the boy and Dick obviously took the hint, for he bit back the words which were hovering on his tongue, and red-faced, attacked the slices of cold mutton on his plate.

Conversation became a little patchy and she was thankful when they all left the room, leaving her with a pile of dirty crockery. She screwed up her nose as she piled them together; no two were alike and many were chipped, all were thick and heavy, and a mental picture of her own delicate china floated into her mind. She discovered two taps over the sink. The water from one was clear, from the other it was slightly discoloured and she guessed that one pipe led from a water tank and that the other was river water. Young Dick came back and volunteered to dry up for her. He confirmed her guess about the taps, explaining briefly that they were not short of water, which was pumped from the river and which was used for baths and washing.

After he had gone she surveyed the kitchen again. The floor would have to be scrubbed and the windows cleaned, also the tins containing the flour and sugar would have to be sifted – she had seen a few weevils when she had peeped in before. Tomorrow, when she officially started work, would do for all that; in the meantime she would pick the sweet peas and find Mr. Kennedy to enquire if he had heard anything of her suitcase. As she moved from the kitchen she glanced down at the print dress. If there was an iron she would be able to wash it through and iron it before she went to bed. But what, in the meantime, could she wear?

Mr. Norton was the first person she met when she was outside. Once again he smiled at her vaguely, and when asked if there was such a thing as an iron, he answered,

"Ask Pat. He knows where everything is, m'dear."

Anne wandered off, looking for the jackaroo. The sun was setting over the paddocks and the breeze had dropped. There was a different feeling in the air with the coming of night and she knew that within half an hour darkness would have fallen and the sky would be alight with a thousand stars. It was all very peaceful and silent, even the birds had ceased their twittering and were settling for the night. She would not be sorry to get into bed either, for she was tired, most probably with the change of air, and bit her lips as she thought of scrambling between the sheets wearing her underclothes.

Pat Kennedy was discovered walking up the track from the paddocks, an unlighted pipe between his teeth. He stopped as she reached him.

"Have you heard any more about my case?" she asked haughtily.

"No sign of it," he answered. "Maybe the mail man will see it on his way out tomorrow."

"Have you made any more enquiries, or are you just taking it for granted that it hasn't been found?"

"Both the chaps I spoke to in town have rung through here," he said with unusual patience. "Neither of them saw anything resembling a suitcase."

"Oh!" Anne bit her lips again. "Is there such a thing as an iron? This dress is dirty –"

"I noticed that."

"If I could wash it through it would soon dry and I could wear it again tomorrow."

"There's a flat-iron in the kitchen."

"Thank you."

Anne discovered it among the cobwebs on the top shelf, half hidden by bars of soap and boxes which rattled when she shook them. Taking a can of hot water and some soap into her room, she locked the door and washed the dress, sitting on the edge of the bed after she had hung it near the window to dry. She felt strangely flat and unhappy, no one seemed to care whether she was comfortable or not and she was not used to being treated as a servant. Which was precisely what she was, of course. Rather longingly she thought of Roddie. He would be preparing to go out, and rather angrily she wondered who would be sitting with him in his rakish sports car.

The warm air dried her dress in a surprisingly short time, leaving it very crumpled and creased, and despairingly she wondered how she could iron it when she had nothing else to put on to go to the kitchen. Her anger shifted to Pat Kennedy – if he had not been so careless she would have had her case and all this would not have happened. It was all his fault. Sitting there with the un-ironed frock in her hands, Sydney seemed very far away.

A cuckoo called persistently and mournfully from a nearby tree, frogs began to croak, and various creatures made rustling noises as they moved through the undergrowth. Anne went to

the window and looked out into the darkness, the fragrance of
the sweet peas wafting over her shoulder into the cool night air.
There was not a light to be seen excepting for the stars, the trees
were outlined against the clear sky, their topmost branches
moving gently in the slight currents of air. The whole world
had changed with the setting of the sun and crumpled dresses
became of little importance. There was no luxury at Gum Valley, unless it was hidden beneath the red roof of the homestead,
but she was confident that when the strangeness wore off and
she became used to the ways of the seven men for whom she
had to cook she would enjoy the freedom of this new life.

There was a tapping on the door and she spun round.

"Who is it?"

"John Norton."

"Just a moment." She scrambled into the crumpled dress,
fastened the buttons and opened the door about half an inch.
"Well?"

"Your nightwear," he said with dignity. "You said you had
nothing to wear." He held out a pair of faded pyjamas. "Mine.
You can borrow them and return them when you find your
own."

"Oh, thank you." She did not wish to prolong the discussion,
neither had she the heart to refuse what was offered. "Thank
you, Mr. Norton."

He stayed there, staring into the room through the small
crack.

"Bed comfortable?" he asked anxiously.

"I don't know yet."

"Nice flowers," he remarked, catching a glimpse of the sweet
peas.

"Yes. Goodnight."

Mr. Norton drew back as a firm footstep sounded in the pas-
sageway. Anne gave a tiny sigh of relief at the sight of the tall
figure which came towards them. Why she was relieved she

did not quite know, for there was certainly nothing to fear from this old man with the saintly-looking face.

"What are you doing here, John?" he asked quietly.

"Giving Miss Smith some nightwear," John Norton explained.

"All right. Now you can go back to your room." Pat Kennedy dismissed him as though the manager was a child, and to Anne's amazement the other said, "Yes, Pat," and vanished from sight.

Pat looked at the girl. "Still staying here?"

"Why not?"

"Because John wanders round all night," he said slowly. "Sometimes he sings, usually he plays a violin. The others are used to it and sleep through whatever noise he makes. That's why I thought – and still think – you would be better in the house."

Anne peered at him round the door. "What *is* all this? Why does Mr. Norton do these things? Is there something wrong with him."

"He had an accident a couple of years ago," he explained. "It had a peculiar effect on him, but you have no need to worry, he's quite harmless and wouldn't hurt a fly. And his memory is very poor."

"So that's why you do everything here?"

He nodded. "Are you coming or not?" he asked impatiently. "I can't wait all night and certainly don't intend coming along every five minutes to see if he's annoying you."

"I'll come," said Anne in a small voice. Perhaps discretion was the better part of valour. In any case she wished to see inside the homestead; if she slept there she would have plenty of good excuses to look round. Opening the door a little wider, she held out the pyjamas. "What can I do with these? They won't fit me for one thing and I don't like pyjamas for another."

"Leave them. We might find something else that will suffice for tonight. If your case doesn't turn up tomorrow you'll have to phone through to town and have them send something out to you." There was no suggestion, she noticed, of her going into town herself to choose what was necessary.

Together they left the building and walked across the thick green lawns after skirting the hedge. There was a faint elusive perfume in the air and Anne lifted her head to sniff, then she remembered something and stopped in the centre of the path.

"I've no money," she cried, and the words had a very odd sound about them.

Pat stopped beside her. "None at all?"

"Only a few coins left in my handbag."

"Is that all you possess?"

She nodded vigorously. "I told you I wanted work." Miss Smith, the cook, would surely let a tear trickle down her cheeks, and one did appear, for the humour of her situation struck her forcibly and they were tears of suppressed laughter that he saw.

"Here, I say! Don't cry, for heaven's sake. I'll lend you some money, give you an advance on your wages if you like. I didn't know things were so bad!"

"They're terrible," sniffed Anne. "All my worldly possessions were in that suitcase, but you were too – too mean to go back and look for it."

"I had no idea –" he began uncomfortably.

"I *told* you."

"You needn't blame me altogether. I didn't lose it."

"It was your fault, you placed it in position. If you'd fastened it on securely it wouldn't have fallen off."

He drew a deep breath, held it and looked for a moment as though he would burst. Then he relaxed.

"Come on," he said roughly. "I ought to have known better than to start arguing with a woman. They never argue logically."

Feeling she had won that round, Anne followed him meekly

along the path, still sniffing the air. The perfume was sweet, strong and familiar.

"I know!" she cried triumphantly, stepping on to the verandah and blinking as he switched on a light. "Orange blossom!"

"What?" Pat Kennedy spun round to look at her.

"I can smell it," she sniffed again. "It smells like a wedding!"

"Don't let it be putting ideas into your head," he warned. "There are a few trees over there." He looked down at the creased dress. "Whatever have you been doing with that?"

"I washed it," she explained. "Then Mr. Norton came to my door and I had to slip it on again. Does it look a sight?"

"Terrible," he said coolly. "There's an iron in here, so you can do it before you go to bed."

So this was Gum Valley, her own house. The hall was wide and thickly carpeted, heavy pictures hung on the walls, and in a sudden panic she wondered if Uncle Claud had any family portraits and if she would be on any of them. Years ago she had seen a lot of him; perhaps he had placed a photograph of his niece in a prominent position. She glanced at the broad back of the man in front of her, trying to imagine what he would have to say if he discovered she was the owner of Gum Valley. It certainly would not be at all complimentary.

The first room she entered was high-ceilinged and cool, the floors were bare of covering and the furniture had been draped with dust covers. Everything was forlorn and rather depressing. Twitching a cover off a chair she examined it carefully. It was old and of good quality, it was also very dusty but looked comfortable.

"When you've quite finished," said the cool voice, "I'll show you your room."

Guiltily the chair was re-covered and Anne followed him further along the hall. There would be time enough for explorations when he was at work and out of the way. The door he opened led into a large bedroom with two long french windows, open now to let in the night air. The double bed stood with its head to one wall and her heart contracted a little. Perhaps it was here that Uncle Claud had said his farewell to the land he loved. There was a dressing table with three mirrors which gave Anne a treble glance at her dishevelled appearance, a huge heavy wardrobe and two chests of drawers. They were all solid and well made; they must have been to withstand the heat through the years without distortion.

Pat Kennedy waited in the doorway until she had finished her inspection.

"The kitchen is along here," he said, standing back and waiting for her.

"Always kitchens," thought Anne viciously. "Miss Smith isn't good enough for anything else!"

The light was switched on and he looked round. "Here's the iron. It's a petrol iron and I don't suppose you know how to start it? No? I'll get it going for you and then keep out of the way until you've finished. In the meantime I'll have a look round and see if there's anything for you to wear until you get something else."

She watched him as he started the iron and when it was going to his satisfaction he gave her a nod and closed the door behind him. What a strange mixture he is, the girl thought as she slipped her dress over her head and laid it on the ironing board, abrupt and rude one minute, thoughtful the next. I rather like him when he laughs and his eyes have a twinkle in them – at times. She could hear him whistling in the distance as he searched through drawers and cupboards looking for something for her to wear. The humour of it all made her laugh again – what a tale she would have to tell her mother when she wrote! A cook, with no money and no clothes, sleeping in her own home with a jackaroo in the room next door. The flat at Rose Bay seemed further away than ever.

The iron worked perfectly and soon the little cotton dress

was spruce and fresh once more. As she was hesitating about putting it on a voice asked if these things would do and putting her hand round the door she grabbed what he was holding out to her and shut it again. The things turned out to be a couple of aprons, a pale blue smock and a pink dressing gown. Anne held them out. They smelled strongly of mothballs and must have belonged to her aunt, the woman who was only a memory.

Wearing the dressing gown and carrying the dress over her arm she sallied forth again. Pat Kennedy called goodnight as she passed his door and she went into her own room, feeling more tired than ever. There was the bed to make, but finally she tumbled into it and hardly had she closed her eyes before she heard a voice calling.

"Pat? Pat?"

Anne sat up, shivering a little. It was the manager, and she hoped he was not going to start singing or playing the violin outside her door. The voices reached her distinctly and she listened, holding her breath.

"What's the matter?" asked the jackaroo.

"Miss Smith has vanished, she's not in her room. Do you know where she is, Pat?"

Anne's heart missed a beat as she waited for the reply.

"I flung her into the river," said the other voice wearily. "Go back to your room, John, and stop this nocturnal prowling."

"Why did you fling her into the river? She was a nice girl."

"She wasn't, and I didn't like her. Now hop it." There was a definite note of command and John Norton bowed to it.

"Yes, Pat."

Anne lay down again. Pat Kennedy might not like her, he had taken no pains to disguise the fact, and she did not like him, but she felt she could trust him. If anything went wrong she had only to call out and he would come immediately to her assistance. With the smell of orange blossom in the room and with a smile round her lips, Anne drifted contentedly off to sleep.

He spoilt everything by banging on the door before six o'clock the following morning.

"Miss Smith! Time to get up. Miss Smith."

"All right, I heard you," snapped Anne crossly. She had been in a deep sleep. She was warm and very comfortable and not at all pleased to be awakened at this early hour.

It was then she discovered she was working for her living. Going out into the cool morning air she looked round with appreciation, wondering if she had ever seen the early morning sky *after* a good night's sleep. Often she had arrived home from a dance or an all-night party about this time, with an aching head and a queer taste in her mouth, too tired to notice the soft colour above or the freshness of the air.

The men were astir, Dick raised a tousled head and called a loud "Good morning" as she passed near his window, and Jan was already in the kitchen when she went in.

"The wood," he smiled at her, and indicated a pile of logs he had brought in, and without a moment's hesitation Anne bent to her task of cleaning out the fire and relighting it. She was not going to give Mr. Kennedy a chance to say anything this morning. The urn was filled with fresh water and placed on the stove and after washing her hands she opened the door of the refrigerator and peered inside. Here she would need some help.

"Jan." She looked at him over the top of the door. "What do you usually have for breakfast?"

The big man came across the kitchen. "Porridge, chops, many chops, yes, toast and tea."

"How many chops?"

"Three, four."

"Each?"

He nodded and Anne did a frantic sum in her head. Four chops for seven men, twenty-eight, and two for herself, for she was hungry this morning – that meant thirty chops.

"Mr. Norton doesn't have his breakfast now," said the other. "He wanders in when he wakes up."

Anxiously the girl looked at the piece of loin she was holding and shook her head. Thirty chops would never come off this. Another glance into the fridge revealed a leg with the chump chops attached and she took them all over to the old table under the window where Jan offered to cut them for her.

"Thank you." She watched him sharpen a knife. "I shall have to learn how to do this, I suppose."

"You certainly will," agreed a voice from the doorway. "Jan won't always be here to cut up the meat for you. The fire is going out. And remind me later to show you how the refrigerator is filled. By the way, we like plenty of good plain food, no fripperies. Has Rusty brought in the milk yet? No? Dick, give him a call, please, he should have finished before this. The chops should be cooking, Miss Smith, or isn't the oven hot enough?"

Rather resentfully Anne stared across the room. Who was he to issue orders like this? Let her get used to the routine here and she would soon show him who was boss in the kitchen. There would be no interference from Mr. Kennedy or anyone else, she was cook and she would let him know it.

The first breakfast was not a success. The porridge was insufficiently cooked and the chops were too brown on one side and not brown enough on the other. But the toast was all right and so was the tea, which vanished in miraculous quantities, so the men forgave her for her mistakes. She was pretty, eager to please and this was the first attempt at cooking in a strange place. Even Pat Kennedy made no comments.

When he had finished he stood up and glanced at Mr. Norton who had made an appearance when the others had nearly finished.

"John, I want you to go into the office, there are some cheques needing your signature."

"Yes, Pat," said Mr. Norton obligingly, and as he had finished a very sparse meal he left the room with the jackaroo.

Rusty snorted. "If Pat told him to jump into the river, he'd just say 'Yes, Pat' and jump in!"

"He has a great deal to thank Pat for, anyway," said Peter in his slow way, and Jan nodded.

"A great deal. He's a hard man to work for, but he's just. We could have someone far worse."

They all watched Pat and Mr. Norton vanish through the hedge and Rusty shrugged his shoulders. He went outside and the others followed, leaving Anne staring at the spot where the manager had disappeared.

An ugly suspicion crossed her mind. Was it possible that when Mr. Norton had had this accident Pat Kennedy had seen the opportunity of feathering his own nest at the expense of the owner of Gum Valley? There was obviously no opposition of any description from Mr. Norton, he did exactly as he was told, as did the men, and there was no one else to counter any orders the jackaroo issued. He was in sole charge and quite at home in the position too, thought Anne viciously. This needed further thought, but there was no sense in rushing it on her first morning. There on the table were dirty pots and she had to wash them, so pushing Pat Kennedy and the subject of Gum Valley's finances to the back of her mind she started to work.

That morning lived in Anne's memory as the worst she had ever lived through. Grimly determined to prepare a decent dinner and to have it ready on time, she worked with one eye on the clock. The huge piece of mutton had to be placed in the oven before she had finished scrubbing the floor, then all the cups and plates had to be washed and the vegetables prepared. There Alan, the gardener, could help her; he would know what they liked best and how much she needed to prepare. But Alan wasn't at all helpful. He resented her presence in his garden and to her enquiry about the vegetables he replied,

"Spuds. Pumpkin. Onions. Beans, peas, whatever's ready."

"And the strawberries?" asked Anne. "Could you pick those and we'll have them for a sweet?"

"Sweet?" Alan straightened his back and glared at her. "We don't have sweets, miss, we have puddens. Hot puddens."

"Oh!" Rather helplessly she gazed at him. "You mean baked puddings?"

"Jam or treacle, or pies. Something sustaining." And as she turned away with her apron full of peas, which had to be shelled, she heard him mutter "*Sweets!*"

The next thing was to fetch the potatoes and pumpkin from the shed, and for those she took a basket. Opening the door she went in slowly. It was dark and cool, and sitting down for a moment on a bag of potatoes, she looked round. The place was well stocked, there were bags of bran and pollard, chicken wheat, seventy-pound bags of sugar and bags of flour and all the numerous things appertaining to food for man, bird and beast.

Popping the potatoes and onions into the basket, Anne had the feeling she was not alone. Someone was watching her and she turned quickly towards the doorway. There was no one there, no shadow either, and for a moment she wondered if one of the numerous dogs had followed her in. You could hear a dog breathe, he would sniff, perhaps brush his tail against a bag. This was no dog. Raising her head, she looked round, then she screamed, a loud penetrating scream, and the next moment she was outside the door, her hand to her throat.

"What on earth's the matter?" asked Pat Kennedy, coming rapidly towards her. "Why are you making all that noise?"

"In there!" Anne gasped. "There's a snake, it was watching me –" she swallowed hard, trying to quieten the frantic beat of her heart.

"Oh, that will be Sammy," he said in a very unconcerned way.

"*Sammy?*"

"He lives in there and feeds off the mice and rats. He's an excellent rat-catcher, far better than a cat."

Slowly Anne lowered her hand. "What kind of a snake is Sammy?" she asked in a trembling voice.

"A carpet snake. And he's quite harmless, I often handle him."

He's laughing at me again, she thought wildly as she met his eyes. He knew that thing was in there when he showed me this place yesterday, he wanted me to go in and discover it for myself.

"Why didn't you tell me he was there? Why didn't you mention it last night when you showed me the shed?" she cried violently. "You might have guessed that I dislike snakes, you knew I'd be frightened and that I'd scream!"

"I must say you didn't disappoint me," he answered thoughtfully.

Speechlessly she gazed at him. Very definitely there was a look of amusement on his face. No retort scathing enough would come to her mind, nothing she could say would take away the memory of her panic. When she did speak her voice shook with rage.

"Mr. Kennedy, I know quite well that you didn't want me to come here. In fact, you've made it perfectly plain. But I'll tell you now that no matter how many snakes you put in my path or however unpleasant you make yourself, you will not drive me away from Gum Valley. I'm here and here I'm staying!"

The amusement died out of his eyes. "Don't delude yourself," he said coldly. "You'll stay at Gum Valley only as long as you do your work properly. If you don't I'll write to Mr. Maynard and explain that you're not satisfactory, and contract or not, you'll go."

"Who says so?" she asked furiously.

"I do. I'm in charge here and don't you forget it!" With that he turned on his heel and left her clutching the basket of onions and potatoes.

CHAPTER FOUR

During the following two weeks Anne had never worked so hard or been so tired. The cooking seemed never-ending and it was a source of great wonder to her that men could eat as these men ate. After the novelty of having a woman cook, and a young and attractive one at that, had worn away, the men began to chaff her and to pass remarks about the food, remarks which sometimes brought a wave of angry colour to her cheeks. To them she was merely Anne Smith, working for her living as they were, and at times their bluntness annoyed her and she longed for the urbane attention of Roddie and his friends. She began to think of him with longing, for he had always been ready with some complimentary remark about her appearance. These men noticed nothing, and yet if they had, womanlike she would have taken it as an insult that they should comment on her appearance.

Perhaps I am in love with him, she thought one morning as she started to peel a huge pile of potatoes, perhaps this was what I need to make me realise how much I miss him.

When, in the evening, she was free at last, all she wanted to do was to creep into her bed and sleep without waking until, just before six, with great regularity, there would come a thump on her door and that hateful voice would shout, "Miss Smith, time to get up."

The tiredness, she realised sensibly, was caused by the sudden change in her way of living and the great difference in the air. The days were warm and cloudless and inclined to languidness, but normally heat did not worry her and she knew she would soon become acclimatized.

There seemed little reward for her labours, even her first two pay cheques, which she received with inner excitement because she had actually earned them, were very small, for she owed a debt to Pat Kennedy for her clothes which she was determined to clear at the earliest possible moment.

With him she was frigidly polite. After the incident of the snake she spoke to him only when necessary and found, to her chagrin, that that state of affairs evidently suited him. She knew he watched her and that he was only waiting for her to make a few more mistakes before writing to Mr. Maynard and asking for the cancellation of her contract.

One evening she ran into him unexpectedly when work was finished and all she had to do now was to go to her room and either read herself to sleep or sit by the window and twiddle her thumbs. There was no one to talk to, the men were sitting on the verandah near their own quarters, laughing together, and she could not join them. As she passed, she noticed the jackaroo was not with them, and acting on a sudden impulse she turned away from the house and walked slowly along the track.

Walking slowly, enjoying her solitude, alternatively watching the changing colours of the sky on the horizon where the sun had set and glancing sideways at the paddocks she wondered about the jackaroo and his connection with Gum Valley. With incredible swiftness it became dark and Anne turned to retrace her steps, halting quickly as she saw the jeep coming towards her. It stopped by her side and Pat leaned out.

"What are you doing out here?"

"Only having a walk," she answered with hauteur, wondering if she had been doing wrong and if he was going to give her another of those cold biting retorts by way of a reply.

"Not tired?"

"Not tonight," she shook her head.

For a moment he hesitated, then leaned over and opened the door.

"In that case, why not come with me? There are a couple of drovers camped on the stock route and I'm taking them some fresh bread and some fruit."

That would be a change, she thought, getting in quickly, for she was becoming tired of doing nothing in the evening. It was a lonely life when there was no one to share anything with her and now she was used to the place she did not feel like rushing off to bed about eight o'clock.

The jeep bounded forward and the headlights flung the track ahead into relief. It all looked very different at night, the trees seemed to alter their shape and become mysterious, the tall brown grass looked thick and somehow treacherous as though it were hiding snakes of all sizes and colours, and thinking of snakes made Anne glance sideways at her companion. There was little to see of his face, just a faint profile with a pipe sticking out from his mouth.

"We start harvesting tomorrow," he announced suddenly.

"You'll be glad to get it over?"

"Too right. It won't take long providing the weather holds and the tractors don't crack up."

Anne looked interested. "Are they in danger of cracking up?"

Pat laughed a trifle grimly. "Miss Smith, those tractors were not new when the Boss was alive, they've worked ever since and despite the care that has been lavished on them they are getting old. We could do with two new ones."

"Well, why haven't two new ones been purchased?" she enquired, and was unprepared for the derisive jeer which followed her question.

"You can ask Miss A.C.S. that one," he retorted in reply.

Her heart missed a beat. Now we might hear why he so dislikes Miss Carrington-Smythe! It might be interesting, and she had not brought the lady into the conversation, he had introduced the subject.

"What has she to do with it?" she wanted to know.

"Everything." The jeep took a corner quickly and straightened out on the rough track again, ahead there was a gleam of fire and Anne sighed; they were nearly at the camp and there was not time for any more serious discussion. And as Pat seemed to consider the subject closed she looked ahead. On either side of the track were sheep, hundreds of sheep, standing huddled together, moving en masse this way and that, baaing continuously and watched by the bright eyes of the dogs. A cart was drawn up alongside the track and two men were sitting by the light of the fire. They hailed the jeep and got quickly to their feet.

"Howdy, Pat!"

"Hullo, mate."

Such were their greetings and Anne looked at them wonderingly. She had never seen drovers before but decided they were no different from the men back at the station. Both were tall and wiry, both wore rather grubby shirts and dusty trousers and perched on the back of their heads were wide-brimmed hats. Nearby came the soft sounds of horses cropping at the grass, and by the flicker of the flames she could see them as they moved to and fro in the shadows.

The men moved to the jeep to get their provisions and noticed her for the first time. Casually Pat introduced her.

"Miss Smith, the station cook."

"Going up in the world, having a young lady to do that for

you!" said one of the drovers with a grin. "How d'you like Gum Valley, miss?"

"I like it very much," Anne smiled as they paused with the loaves of bread in their arms. "It's so quiet and peaceful."

"I reckon it is," answered one thoughtfully. "But if it's quietness you want you'd better come with us. Two hundred miles we've brought this lot and never a town we've been through. The only trouble is that Harry here talks too much!"

The man beside him chuckled. "I've spoken to him three times today."

"Breakfast, lunch and now," nodded his companion, and they looked at each other in great understanding and friendliness. They would need to be friendly, thought Anne, watching them move towards the fire again, riding two hundred miles behind a mob of sheep, spending long evenings together with only their dogs and horses for company. As she looked at the three men she remembered Roddie, trying to picture him in these surroundings, and smile faintly.

"Like a cuppa?" asked an enquiring voice, and she nodded at the sight of a battered billycan.

It was more than peaceful sitting on the edge of the cart, swinging her bare legs and drinking strong milkless tea in the flickering light of the fire, in company with these three men of the bush. Not for anything would she be back in Sydney now, rushing about preparing for a party or a dance, listening to Barbara's needless chatter and the excited giggles of the other girls. It was far nicer, she decided dreamily, looking at the fire through half-closed eyes, to be Miss Smith, sitting on a cart on a stock route with three quiet-voiced men and getting sleepier and sleepier every minute. The wisest thing she could have done was to come out West.

Pat glanced at her and got to his feet.

"Miss Smith, we'd better be going. You have to be up at six, you know."

Her head jerked up quickly. Why had he to spoil everything by reminding her of that?

It was when they were nearly back at the staiton she remembered she still had to iron a dress in the morning and she sighed. Having only three dresses did have its advantages, there was no puzzling about what to wear, but it had its disadvantages too. A clean one was necessary every day and when, as she had done at dinner time, split some gravy down the front, it meant another change and the rotation was spoilt.

"Would you mind getting the petrol iron going for me?" she asked when they reached the gate. "The fire will be out, so I can't use the flat iron and I must press my dress."

"All right," he said wearily, and the tone of his voice gave her the feeling she was a nuisance.

In the kitchen of the homestead he looked at her. "If you're still short of clothes why don't you make yourself some? There's a sewing machine out there, probably needs oiling, but I'll fix it up for you."

"I never thought of that," said Anne weakly. How on earth did one make clothes? How did you start, what did you do?

Pat was watching her – was there a challenging light in his eyes?

"Of course I'll make something," she exclaimed stoutly. "But I have no material –"

"I'm going into town one day this week –"

"You will certainly not choose a pattern or the material," she cried. "That's something I must do myself. There are other things I need, too," she added quickly. "Such as powder – I haven't powdered my nose since the day I arrived!"

Pat smiled as he started the iron. "That's not a tragedy, Miss Smith. However, if you want to go into town I think we can manage it one day soon. Can you drive a car?"

That was something she *could* do. "Certainly. I've had a licence for the past seven years."

"As long as that?" he raised his eyebrows and she flushed.

"There's no need to be rude, Mr. Kennedy –" she began heatedly, but he interrupted her.

"I wasn't being rude. On the contrary, I was paying you a compliment. I didn't think you were old enough to have had a licence for so long."

"Oh!" To her annoyance the flush deepened. Somehow one did not associate compliments with this man. "Thank you."

So, for the first time, they said goodnight in charity with one another and Anne surpassed herself at breakfast time the following morning, everything was ready on time and it was all well cooked.

Peter was a horribly silent man. At one period Anne wondered if he was dumb, he would sit throughout a meal and not say a single word, no matter how energetic an argument was in progress across the table. Then he said "Thank you" one evening when she handed him something and she discovered he did have a tongue. Even when the jackaroo gave his instructions and orders of the day Peter would listen, incline his head and disappear, and she guessed because he was the one of them who never caught the sharp edge of Mr. Kennedy's tongue that he did all he was expected to do in the correct manner.

With Rusty she was wary. She disliked him and the way his eyes would linger upon her and the way he smiled at her. Dick remarked one evening that Rusty always thought himself a lady-killer, he was forever boasting about his girl-friends in town, and Anne, having no wish to be classed as one of those, kept out of his way as much as it was possible to do. It was not always easy, and when she did wander on the river bank after the evening meal she got into the habit of asking either Dick or Jan to accompany her. The latter made himself useful in an unobtrusive way. He was a gentle and kindly soul and his delight one afternoon, when she answered him in faultless German, made her smile.

"You have travelled?" he asked in his own language, and Anne nodded. Then the need for caution came into her mind. It would never do tell him how much she had travelled.

"Not very far," she said, and added, "I had a German teacher once and picked up the language very quickly."

"That is good indeed," he beamed at her with great good humour.

Once or twice after that she would make some comment to him in German when she did not wish the others to know what she was saying and forgot herself one morning when she drew his attention, with a very uncomplimentary remark, to the fact that Mr. Kennedy had come to the breakfast table with yesterday's growth of hair on his chin. Immediately Pat's face went red and he spun round in his chair, telling her with an accent as perfect as her own, that he would shave in his own good time and it was of no concern of hers. Jan, the only man who could follow the rapid flow of words, laughed outright, partly because of Anne's discomfiture and partly because he had forgotten to warn her that Pat knew not only German but French as well.

One weekend Dick accompanied her down to the river and they sat in the shade of the bank with fishing lines held slackly in their hands. It was he who led the conversation, born in the Western Districts. He had never been far from Murra Creek and wanted to know a great deal about Sydney and Brisbane, Anne's birthplace. She kept a watch on her tongue; it would have been so easy to describe some of the numerous places she had visited abroad. In turn she wanted to know more about Gum Valley, but there she found him strangely uncommunicative. He discussed the land and the harvest, which they had started to gather in, but he would not discuss either Mr. Norton or Pat Kennedy.

"I believe you've got a bite," he said, tactfully changing the subject after one or two very pointed questions, and she drew in the line. Beside her the boy gave a whoop of delight when he unhooked quite a sizeable fish. Anne looked at it and wrinkled her nose.

"Somehow I don't fancy eating a fish that's never seen the sea."

"They're good," exclaimed Dick. "I hope we get some more, they'll make a change for tea. That is, if you can cook fish."

"Of course I can cook fish!" she cried indignantly. "What made you think I couldn't?

He grinned at her, an engaging grin which made him look like an overgrown schoolboy. "Don't be mad at me," he pleaded. "But sometimes the meat is tough and the cakes you make are rather hard."

"Oh!" Anne was startled by this candour.

"Pat said you need more routine in the kitchen –"

"He did, did he?" asked Miss Smith, drawing in her breath. "He's been discussing me behind my back?"

"No," answered Dick quickly, looking at her uncertainly. "Pat hasn't discussed you with us all, but I overheard him telling Mr. Norton one morning that you were doing a bit better than he'd expected, but you needed more routine, sometimes the meals were not ready on time. And time is precious at the moment – we want to get the wheat in before it either rains or some thoughtless person drops a cigarette end somewhere and starts a fire."

The criticism was true, Anne had to admit it, for she still could not time everything to be ready altogether. Some mornings the meat was ready long before the vegetables, sometimes the puddings were insufficiently baked when the time came to take them out of the oven. This job was not as easy as she had thought it was going to be, cooking for seven men meant much thought, and up to now she had gone about her tasks with a kind of grim gaiety. These men did not want grimness, neither did they require gaiety, all they asked for and all she was paid to do was for well-cooked meals to be placed before them at certain intervals. Anne stared down at the water, feeling a wave of self-pity sweep over her. She was a stranger to this kind of work, they should make more allowances for her inexperience.

"You've another bite," Dick interrupted her thoughts, and hastily she pulled once more on the line. At the sight of the squirming fish her courage returned. She had come up here of her own accord, determined to work, and she would do it. In the homestead there must be old cookery books of her aunt's which would help her considerably; she would search for them some time when Pat Kennedy was not about, and study them.

"We'll have a lovely tea tonight," she promised as Dick unhooked her catch. "If we catch sufficient."

"Not much use me trying," he grumbled. "Nothing's touched my line yet. Oh, here's Pat."

The jackaroo was coming along the river bank towards them and Anne looked at him coolly as he joined them. He nodded and sat down beside Dick, stretching out his long legs with a sigh of thankfulness.

"Got that job finished?" asked the youngster curiously.

"Yes, thank heaven. How I wish we could wangle another tractor!"

Dick darted a smiling glance at him. "Maybe this harvest will bring its own reward."

"Maybe," answered Pat, smiling too. "But the whole thing is getting me down." He lay back and cradled his head on his bent arms. "Caught anything?" he asked Anne lazily.

"Two. We're going to have a fish tea tonight for a change."

"That will be nice," he agreed rather absently.

He looks tired, she thought suddenly. While Dick and I have been sitting here in comfort he's been struggling with one of the tractors trying to keep it in trim for the harvest. At night he worked in the small office until long after she went to bed. What did he do in there, and why did he keep the door locked during the daytime so no one else could go in? She remembered the suspicion she had had, that he was carefully and systematically robbing her. Someone was doing it, that was quite obvious from what she had learnt from Mr. Maynard; it was equally obvious that no one else in this isolated place had any chance to tamper with the accounts. Mr. Norton obligingly signed the cheques when requested to do so and that was all he was paid to do; for the rest of the day he dozed placidly in the shade and at night he played his violin in the distance. Once or twice when he had wandered into the kitchen during the day, she had questioned him carefully about one thing or another, but his stock answer to anything seemed to be,

"Ask Pat, m'dear, he knows everything."

Pat did seem to know everything. All that happened on the property came to his notice. Anne had heard his enthusiasm about the high yield of the wheat when he had been discussing the harvest with the other men and the drivers of the trucks who took the bagged wheat to the railway. They had teased him and said if Gum Valley continued to produce such good crops he would be retiring shortly.

Anne looked around. The river was placid and still at her feet, the gum trees on either bank dipped motionless boughs towards the water and overhead the sky was a brilliant unbelievable shade of blue. The land was prolific – she had only to look at Alan's garden to discover that. Tomatoes were growing strongly, tied to their stakes, the pumpkins, marrows and squashes were covering the soil with a carpet of green as they spread in all directions, the strawberries were large and luscious, and all the other common vegetables were healthy and large. It was a rich land, watered from the river at her feet, and yet – she looked again at the face of the man beside her.

Somehow he did not seem the type to do such a thing. He was above the others in his outlook, his speech and his bearing, he was just in his dealings with the station hands and wonderfully gentle with John Norton. At the same time he was ruthless, and she could well imagine that once he had set his mind on anything he would go to any length to get it. He was unpredictable occasionally sarcastic and bad-tempered, also he seemed to enjoy taunting her. Never, she thought viciously, would she forgive him for losing her case or for not telling her about the snake in the store shed. A man who would deliberately keep silent about such a thing for the sole purpose of frightening her was quite capable of doing anything else, such as altering the accounts of Gum Valley to suit himself. Aware that her thoughts were contradicting themselves, she turned her attention to her fishing line which was taut, and in silence she drew in another fish.

Glancing at Dick, she saw that he had fallen asleep and in his sleep he looked a mere child. Rather than ask Pat to help her she started gingerly to try and unhook the fish, it wriggled in her grasp and nearly fell back into the river, Anne tightened her grip with an inward shudder and tried to pull out the hook.

"Want any assistance?" enquired Pat, rolling over to watch her.

"No, thank you."

Well aware of his cool scrutiny, she struggled the harder to get the hook from the mouth of the struggling fish. He'll be laughing at me again in a moment, she thought, tugging angrily at both the fish and the hook, and I suppose I really do look funny. His eyes were filled with genuine amusement as he watched her unavailing efforts.

"You'll pull it apart if you go on like that much longer," he observed casually, and she glanced at him with dislike.

"It's all very well for you to lie there and pass comments," she cried. "But the thing is stuck –"

"Naturally. That's the idea of a fishing hook."

"There!" The hook parted company with the fish and caught in the flesh of Anne's palm. She gave an involuntary cry of pain and instantly a hand grasped her wrist and with great gentleness the hook was removed.

"You are obstinate, aren't you?" he asked as he wrapped her hand in his handkerchief. "You should have let me take it off for you in the first place. Come up to the house and I'll clean it for you." She opened her lips, intending to say she was quite capable of doing it for herself, but he forestalled her. "Yes, I know you can do it, Miss Smith, but we're thirty-two miles from a doctor and I want to know it's done right. I don't want a case of blood poisioning added to all my other worries."

Leaving Dick still fast asleep on the river bank they walked over the grass towards the homestead. In the kitchen she was made to bathe her hand, then Pat advanced across the room with a small bottle. Without a word he lifted her wrist and poured raw iodine into the open cut. Anne winced and drew in her breath sharply, then she bit her lip and felt the tears sting her eyes.

"Is that all you had?" she gasped accusingly, and he nodded.

"I'm sorry, but you can't be too careful. Is it still stinging?"

Her eyes were blurred with tears and she felt his hand on her shoulder, gripping it hard. Gradually she relaxed and gave a watery smile.

"Thank you, Mr. Kennedy."

"That's quite all right, Miss Smith," he said formally, holding out a bandage, and she allowed him to bind up her hand.

"Dick will be disappointed if he doesn't have fish for tea. I don't – don't see how I can manage to fillet it with this on."

"Perhaps Jan will cook it. It might be better in any case if he does do it," said Pat, looking at her thoughtfully.

"Why?" she demanded, and he drew back after snipping the ends of the bandage with a small pair of scissors.

"We have fish so rarely it would be a shame to spoil it," he explained.

"Oh!" One moment he was a comfort – he would never know how the grip of his hand on her shoulder had kept her from crying out when the iodine worked its way into the open cut – the next moment he was his cool awkward self again. "Mr. Kennedy –"

"Yes, Miss Smith?"

"I'm well aware that the meals haven't always been all they should have been –" Anne stopped. What on earth am I saying? she thought. I will not apologise to him for *anything*.

"I'm also aware that you haven't been a cook before, so there's some excuse," he answered, and she spun round to face him, her heart pounding.

"What gave you that idea?" she asked quickly.

"Why, your cooking," he said amiably, putting the bandage neatly into the first-aid box.

It was unfortunate that Anne had forgotten to attend to the refrigerator, for when she opened the door on the Monday morning, preparatory to getting breakfast, she discovered it had defrosted itself and the chops were lying in a pool of discoloured water. The butter had melted and the milk was sour, and in consternation she stared down at the mess before her. Before she had time to shut the door and call Jan, who would have done his best to help her out of this predicament, Pat was standing behind her, surveying everything with his cool grey eyes.

"When did you last attend to this?" he asked, and Anne thought wildly that if only the fridge was as cold as his voice she would not have had anything to worry about.

"Thursday morning, I think," she answered in confusion, well aware that the fault was hers.

"And now it's Monday." He drew a deep breath and then unleashed his fury. Anne cowered back against the refrigerator as he stormed at her, telling her she was incompetent, that he had known a female cook would surely spoil everything at Gum

Valley and the sooner she departed the better the men, and himself in particular, would be pleased.

Anne quivered. Never had anyone spoken to her as Pat Kennedy was speaking to her now. Because of her wealth and position people had always spoken to her with respect, but there was certainly no respect in his voice or on his face as he upbraided her for her carelessness.

Stung by his unreasonable attitude, her own fiery temper flared up and she started to answer him back, the two of them then indulged in a hot wordy battle, which made the men grin discreetly behind their hands.

It was on the tip of Anne's tongue to reveal her identity and dismiss the jackaroo on the spot, and the words might have tumbled from her trembling lips if Pat had not turned away from her with an angry shrug of his shoulders and strode out into the open air.

In the kitchen Anne continued to stand before the refrigerator, a hand to her throat as she waited for her heart to stop its rapid beating and to wonder why she let that man upset her to such an extent.

Her mood of depression lightened in the afternoon. Pat had not come in for his meal and she did not enquire where he was, but gathered from the conversation of the others that there was more trouble with the tractor and he was out in the middle of a paddock in the blazing sun trying to rectify matters. "And it serves him right," she thought resentfully. "I hope he frizzles!"

The mail van arrived shortly after two o'clock, being an ordinary utility which contained an assortment of parcels. The first time Anne had seen its arrival she had laughed outright. There were large parcels of bread, one or two boxes of groceries, a bundle of plants and a case of oranges all mixed up with the bags of mail for delivery at the various places on the long tedious round. This afternoon the mail for Gum Valley included a bulky envelope for her. She recognised Mr. Maynard's writing and by the feel of it there were two or three letters enclosed. She noticed all the correspondence for the station was put on one side for Pat's attention. Mr. Norton received nothing and did not even bother to open one envelope of those addressed to the manager. Among them she glimpsed one letter from the local bank and another from the firm of Maynard, Maynard and Jeen, the solicitors. That intrigued her, and the knowledge that she would never get to know what was written there irritated her. After all, it was her property and she had every right to know what was going on.

But first of all there was her own correspondence. The envelope revealed a letter from her mother, another from Roddie, two more from friends and a short one from Mr. Maynard himself. This she read first.

It began very formally. "Dear Miss Smith. You will appreciate the reason for the abrupt mode of address and hope you will forgive me. Thank you for your letter, which interested me considerably, your description of Gum Valley and of the men working there was very clear and precise. I was very shocked and surprised to learn that Mr. Norton suffered an accident and has been superseded by the jackaroo, who, from your observations, appears to be the root of our troubles. This definitely needs more attention – unfortunately Mr. Jeen, who was due to return from his holiday two weeks ago, is now suffering from measles." Here Anne chuckled. She had met Mr. Jeen on more than one occasion and he struck her as being the very last person to suffer from measles. "However, if you do not mind continuing to watch out for further discrepancies, I will talk everything over with my partner as soon as he is out of quarantine and then, perhaps, the best thing for us to do is to go through the accounts once again and when those are audited we will both come to Gum Valley and straighten things out once and for all."

Anne put down the letter and stared out towards the river.

Mr. Maynard had got the wrong idea altogether, she thought crossly. She had not come up here in the first place to look for discrepancies, she had come to work, to give herself some satisfaction out of life. It had not been as easy as she had imagined it to be, but if she left out the arguments and rows with the jackaroo, she could say with great honesty that she liked the life and that she had settled down in a surprisingly short time. If Mr. Maynard and Mr. Jeen came up here and had things out with the manager and his assistant everything would end. She frowned as she replaced the letter in the envelope and opened the one from her mother.

Mrs. Smythe had been equally as interested in the description of Gum Valley and its occupants. She made one or two sly digs at her daughter's continued references to Pat Kennedy, saying he sounded most interesting and it really might be worth her while to come and have a look at him. "However, if I do come, rest assured that I shall keep your secret, you shall continue to be Miss Smith the cook and I shall give my orders to you accordingly."

Anne laughed and hoped that her mother would arrive unexpectedly one day.

The letter from Roddie was tender and reminiscent. He said he missed her and that he was longing for her to return to Sydney and her ordinary way of living. After reading it, Anne did not feel in any way down-hearted because he was so far away; in fact, she privately thought the letter was a trifle insipid and surprised at her thoughts tried to conjure up a picture of him in her mind. Roddie refused to materialise; instead there was a picture of a tall dark man sweating in the sun as he bent over a broken tractor, and annoyed with herself, she gathered together her letters and scurried away.

When she was free in the evening she stood by the kitchen door and hesitated. She was tired of her own company and wanted to sit somewhere other than her bedroom. It would have been pleasant to go for a walk, but after glancing round she noticed neither Jan nor Dick were in sight. Rusty was there, however, and catching her eye strolled across to join her.

"Finished for the day?" he asked cheerily, and the girl nodded. "How about a stroll on the river bank?"

"No, thanks," she said hastily.

"Why not?" he asked rather truculently. "You go with Dick and Jan, so why not with me?"

"I've some washing to do," she temporised, and drew back as he put his hand on her arm.

"Aw, come on, Anne. It's a lovely evening, the washing can wait."

His hand felt hot and his eyes as he looked down at her seemed to glitter. Anne shivered, for she had never liked him. He moved nearer to her and looked down into her face.

"We'll just stroll," he promised with a laugh. "And come back whenever you want. Surely you aren't afraid of me?"

"Of course not!" she exclaimed quickly. "But I've told you —"

"Rusty!" A bellow came from across the kitchen garden. "Come here a moment."

Rusty spun round and frowned. "Damn Pat," he muttered. "I thought he was still messing about with that tractor!"

As he turned to answer the summons Anne sped away, thankful that the jackaroo had returned and had seen the way Rusty was pestering her.

In the homestead she stopped in the hall and looked round. The poor house was desolate; it needed a bit of life putting into it. It was her house now and it was her own fault it was so silent — she should have come here years before to put it in order. And as she needed somewhere other than her bedroom and the kitchen to spend her spare time she would start immediately to make herself more comfortable. Let Mr. Kennedy say what he liked, she would be quite prepared this time for his display of anger!

Wandering through the rooms, she decided most of them were too big. A number of people were needed to make them hospitable. What she required was a small room, and she recollected that there was one. Evidently her aunt had used it once as a sitting-room, for it opened out on to the verandah and faced the river. Opening the door she peeped inside and gave a sigh of content. This would do nicely for her purpose. For the next hour she was very busy. The windows were opened to let in the breeze and blow out the fustiness, the dust-covers were removed from the furniture and the rugs were taken outside and thoroughly shaken.

Armed with a pair of scissors she went into the garden and proceeded to cut a large bunch of flowers.

When the flowers were arranged she stood back to admire the result. The room was cool and inviting, a perfect haven for a weary soul at the end of a busy day, for it beckoned you to sit down and relax.

When Pat came into the house, tired and disheartened, for the tractor refused to start despite all he and the others had done to it, he could not see the usual line of light from beneath the door of Miss Smith's room. He frowned, wondering if Rusty had managed to coax the girl to go for a walk with him. Gently he tapped on the door and received no reply, so he tapped again, then peeped in. The room was empty and Miss Smith was not in bed.

His frown deepened. Surely she had more sense than to go walking with the groom along the river bank after dark. He knew what Rusty was and he certainly did not like the idea.

"Oh, drat the girl!" he muttered, and paused. There was a light coming from the room Mrs. Carrington-Smythe had used. Surely Miss Smith had not had the effrontery to go in there?

In the doorway he stopped. Miss Smith had made herself very much at home, for she was lying on the settee wearing some flimsy thing he had not seen before, she was reading the weekend papers which had come out with the mail man and on a small table by her side was a cut-glass bowl filled with apricots. Her head was resting on a large cushion and her feet were curled up under her. Hardly able to credit his eyes, Pat glanced quickly round the room. There were bowls of roses, sweet peas and fern, the piano was open and a pile of magazines were on the arm of a chair.

"What in the name of Hades do you think you're doing?" he stuttered.

Anne did not raise her head. She had heard him come in and with her heart beating rather loudly she was waiting for the storm to burst.

"Reading," she murmured.

"I can see that," he snapped. "Miss Smith, who gave you permission to do this?"

"Do what?" she enquired provokingly.

"Alter the furniture, take possession of this room. Hang it all, woman, it's not your house!"

"Neither is it yours," she retorted. Putting down the paper she sat up and looked at him over the end of the settee. "Mr. Kennedy, I think I have as much right as you to make myself comfortable. You use the big bedroom, the office, the bathroom and the kitchen. As the office door is always locked, and anyway I have no desire to sit in there in the evening, I think I'm entitled to use this room. I'm not hurting anything here and I'm very comfortable," she finished, lowering her eyes. "Surely you don't expect me to spend my life in either a kitchen or a bedroom."

Pat bit his lip, for he could see her point of view.

"No one will ever know," she said softly, and an unwilling smile crept into his eyes.

"You're right," he agreed suddenly. "Why shouldn't we make ourselves at home? Miss A. C. S. doesn't care. After all, why not?"

He looked round the room again and turned away. Anne lay down feeling slightly disappointed. She had been all ready for fireworks and none had come.

A quarter of an hour later Pat rejoined her and she put her hand over her mouth. He had evidently shaved and had a shower, for he was wearing a clean white shirt and on his bare feet were a pair of slippers. He smiled as he passed her and pulled a chair nearer to the empty fireplace, so it was more convenient for him to put his feet up against the mantelpiece, and with his pipe in his mouth he reached across for one of the papers. After that there was silence for a while. Anne studied the society pages of the Sunday paper and noticed one or two items about friends of hers. One was to be a bridesmaid at a big wedding and there was a description of the dress she was going to wear.

It seemed such a trivial thing, Anne thought, and after all, the majority of people were not interested. To her own knowledge this girl had been a bridesmaid four times within the past twelve months and she remembered with a smile all the flutter of excitement this girl had been in when the photographers had arrived. Did I ever pose like that? she asked herself.

"I hope not!" she muttered.

"What?"

Her head jerked round. "I was muttering to myself," she said, indicating the paper. "What things they do print in here!"

Pat glanced across and nodded his head. "I agree. Not that I read such things, I don't, but I have no time for society girls."

"Why?"

"Because the owner of this place is one," he answered harshly.

"You can't judge her when you've never met her," said Anne slowly.

"Miss Smith, you can judge a person by their actions, even if you don't meet them personally. Miss A. C. S. has owned Gum

72

Valley for about four years, and during that time she's never written one word to either John or myself, she hasn't been near the place, and whenever I've written with some query, the letter has always been answered by the solicitor. On one occasion she was in the United States when we wanted permission to do something and the solicitor refused to allow us to carry on with our plans. On another occasion I was told she was in England, and during the floods two years ago, Miss Carrington-Smythe was in Europe and upon her return there was no enquiry as to how we had fared or what damage was done. As long as she gets the money that's all that seems to matter to her. And heaven knows but she's had plenty since she inherited the place."

"Has she?" asked the girl weakly, feeling about the size of sixpence under the scorn in his voice.

"Too right! And not one penny has come back into the place. We need new tractors, a new water pump, we need dozens of things. Because she's nothing but an empty-headed society butterfly, with dozens of hangers-on all eager to help her spend her money, do you wonder I despise her, although I've never met her? Pah!" He looked at her moodily and Anne lowered her eyes, alarmed at the vehemence in his voice. Then he laughed. "I'm sorry, I shouldn't take it out of you. It's not your fault. And I was rather rude to you this morning."

"I deserved it," replied a very chastened Anne. She was not thinking of the refrigerator but of all the things he had said; Miss Carrington-Smythe had not written to Gum Valley since she had inherited the property, she had ignored its existence until she had acquired a sudden longing to work and to leave Sydney. The truth hurt, but at the same time there were many things which needed sorting out and clearing up. Pat had remarked that the money from Gum Valley had been spent on her pleasures, but that was not true. She thought of the little office with the locked door, of Mr. Norton being paid for dozing in the sunshine, and at the same time she thought of the way this man worked from daylight until dusk. Where *did* the fault lie?

Pat had offered his apology, she had accepted it and he was satisfied. That, therefore, was the end of the matter.

"By the way, I oiled the sewing machine for you and it's ready any time you want to use it. Would you like to go into town on Thursday?"

"Yes. Yes, I'd like to," said Anne, rather bewildered by the change of tone in his voice.

"I'll go in early in the morning on one of the trucks taking in the wheat and you can follow later in the jeep. There's no need to worry about losing your way as long as you remember to turn right when you get off our track."

"That was about six miles from here, wasn't it?"

"That's right. Just keep going on that road and you'll be O.K. I'll meet you in town somewhere and we'll come back together when you have finished your shopping."

He picked up the paper again, settled himself more comfortably in his chair and became silent.

Despite the companionship of the evening his manner was abrupt again the following morning and Anne was treated once more as Miss Smith, the cook. Pat hardly spoke to her at meal times and when he did so there was in his voice a slight mocking tone which so annoyed her.

He vanished into the office that evening and Anne heard the slow tap-tap of a typewriter. Dearly she would have loved to peep in to watch him, but that would bring another shower of abuse upon her head and at the moment she did not feel like an argument. She was worried about the sewing machine. It was ready, cleaned and oiled, but she had not the faintest idea as to what she had to do with it. Tentatively she moved the wheel, consequently the needle moved up and down. So much for that, but where did the material go, and wasn't she supposed to put cotton in somewhere? The faint tap-tap continued from the office, so she fetched a bundle of rags from the kitchen, found a reel of black cotton, and after drawing up a chair sat down to work it out.

After the end of ten minutes she leaned back and surveyed it balefully. It just wouldn't work. No matter what she moved or adjusted, the piece of rag merely slid about under the needle and the cotton was loose and hung in loops. Why, she asked herself crossly, hadn't using a sewing machine been included in her very expensive education?

Still struggling to manipulate everything all at once, she was conscious of Pat standing behind her and she turned quickly in her chair.

"What's the matter? Won't it work?"

"Of course! That is, I think so." Desperately she racked her brains for an excuse and then said with dignity, "You see, it's so very different from any machine I've used before!"

"Oh!" He glanced at her oddly. "I thought all sewing machines worked on more or less the same principle. You haven't got the cotton in right for a start. It goes so. Through there, down there, now thread the needle." Anne did as she was told with great meekness. He was leaning over her shoulder, big and strong and somehow comforting. "Now where's a piece of material? You put it there, let down that little catch and the thing works."

Strangely enough it did, and as her feet worked the treadle so the even stitches began to form. "I'll leave it as it is," she thought. "And then tomorrow I'll use it again and get the hang of it." Turning her head, she looked up into his face. "How long have you been using sewing machines?" she asked innocently.

"Don't get me wrong," he answered quickly. "I merely like tinkering with gadgets."

Anne snatched an hour the following afternoon to tinker

on the rags. She felt a glow of pride as she looked at them. This was going to be extremely useful; once she got the hang of it she would be able to make all kinds of things. After that she sat down to write to her mother, and when Mrs. Smythe received it she read it through twice with a smile round her lips and then sat staring into space, very busy with her thoughts.

CHAPTER FIVE

THURSDAY MORNING DAWNED bright and clear and Anne, as she crossed from the homestead to the kitchen, wondered why she was so excited at the prospect of going into town. With a sense of shock she realised that during the weeks she had been at Gum Valley she had not spoken to another woman. She had not stirred from within a mile or so of the house, excepting for the night she had gone with Pat to meet the drovers, and that the thought of her isolation did not worry her at all.

As she placed the chops on each plate and put a couple of fried eggs on each, she was busy planning how she would spend the few pounds she possessed. Throughout the meal she was silent and preoccupied and Dick twitted her about her absent manner.

"There seems to be a lot to plan," she excused herself. "There's a meal to prepare for you and a list of groceries to make out. Also, I want so many things myself."

By ten o'clock she had prepared the vegetables and made a cold sweet. Jan came in with a huge leg of mutton which he carefully placed in a large baking dish and told her to get ready.

"You leave everything, I'm cook today," he said. "Pat left early with one of the trucks, and," he glanced at her quickly, "Rusty is going in with you."

"Why?" she spun round, annoyed.

"He says he's ready for a day off. Anne, you drive –"

"I will," she promised grimly, wishing the groom had chosen another day to have his day off.

When she was ready and went to the jeep she found Rusty hanging nonchalantly against the door, and piled into the back were many fruit boxes.

"Whatever are those?" asked Anne in amazement.

Lazily the groom stood upright. "Apricots. We'll leave them at the station, here's the consignment note."

"The station?" Anne looked bewildered. "Why?"

"We send them away," was the explanation. "There's been a wonderful crop this year and it's a shame to let them go to waste, so Pat said we might as well sell them. Should get a good price for them, too!"

"And who gets the cash?" she asked.

He grinned. "We all do. We share it, sort of bonus."

"I see!" said Miss Smith, and beat him to the driving seat.

So they stripped the fruit trees, sold the fruit and divided the proceeds among themselves, she thought viciously as she sped away in a cloud of dust. Did they do the same with the peaches, grapes and oranges as they ripened? The money received for the fruit should have been entered into the station's books, and it was all the jackaroo's doing.

"You look mad," remarked Rusty.

"I am."

"With me?"

"With you. With Mr. Kennedy. Oh, with all of you!" she exclaimed.

But it was too pleasant a day to be annoyed for long and there were many questions she wanted to ask about the surrounding countryside, questions which had hovered on her tongue during the first drive out to Gum Valley. Rusty would be only too glad to talk, whereas Mr. Kennedy either answered in monosyllables or did not speak at all.

"What are those marks round the trunks of the trees?" she asked, glancing to one side of the track where it dipped slightly.

"The marks of water during the last flood."

Anne was startled. "Surely not! The marks are at least six feet above the ground."

"The track dips here," he explained. "And the river is just over there." He waved his hand towards the belt of trees which bordered the bank. "When the water came over it settled here and then raced across country. We were cut off from the town for nearly three weeks."

"Do you often have floods?"

"Not very often. Although you can never tell what will happen, a lot depends on how much rain they have back stream."

"It's a pity the station is so near the river bank," she remarked, and Rusty snorted.

"There would be no station at all if it wasn't for the river. Where would we get water out here? Over three hundred miles from the sea. Everything depends on the river."

Anne hadn't thought of that. She pictured the pioneers after their weary trek, first over the mountains and then across the plains, choosing a spot near the life-giving water for the new homes.

"Are you having lunch with Pat?" he asked suddenly, and she answered before she knew what she was doing.

"Of course not!"

"Good! Will you have it with me, then?"

There was no excuse she could advance, for she knew no one in the township and the shopping she had to do would not keep her occupied all the time. So she slowly nodded her head and Rusty smiled.

Upon entering the township he began to whistle softly under his breath, anticipating a hectic few minutes when Pat discovered he had taken the day off and driven into town with the girl. Sure enough, as they passed the large store, which sold everything from tractors and refrigerators to pins and salt, someone stepped from the kerb and Anne drew up quickly.

Pat did not glance at her; through narrowed eyes he was watching the groom.

"Who gave you permission to come into town today?"

"Aw, don't look like that, Pat. I haven't had a day off for ages."

"You aren't paid to have days off."

"I'll forgo my pay for today," Rusty grinned. "It's worth it to have Anne lunch with me."

The girl squirmed a little on the hard seat. She peeped at Pat, he looked livid as he asked harshly,

"Are you dining with him?"

"He asked me," she said, a trifle defiantly.

"I see." That was all. "All right, Rusty, you can take those cases to the station and I'll meet you both here about four o'clock. Order the groceries you need, Miss Smith, order them early and they'll be ready when we are. And Rusty –" he looked at him coldly, "if you dare have more than two beers this afternoon you won't return with us to Gum Valley."

"O.K.," said Rusty sulkily, moving into the driving seat as Anne dropped lightly to the ground.

Pat did not stay with her and as the jeep moved away Rusty shouted he would meet her at the Post Office at half past twelve.

Walking slowly along the main street with its wide overhanging verandahs and sun-blinds, she looked in all the windows and peered round with interest. There was a plentiful selection of everything. Murra Creek was by no means out of date or behind the times with the goods for sale and in some cases the articles were cheaper than they were in Sydney.

Passing a hairdressers, she put her hand up to her head feeling the uneven ends. By the time she came out into the sunshine it was nearly one o'clock and in the distance Rusty could be seen waiting outside the Post Office, looking anxiously up and down the road.

Rather to Anne's surprise, he proved to be quite an entertaining companion, perhaps a trifle loud in his speech, but very proud to have her with him. The conversation was kept on a common level; she soon discovered that, like Dick, he refused to discuss affairs out at Gum Valley.

"But Mr. Norton?" she asked, puzzled, when they were sitting over their coffee. "What happened when he had his accident? Why did Mr. Kennedy take over the place?"

Rusty glanced at her suspiciously. "You seem very curious, Anne."

"I *am* curious," she confessed, and gave him a dazzling smile. "What woman wouldn't be?"

He nodded, as though that explained everything. "Mr. Norton was accidentally shot one day while we were all out shooting rabbits. He was in hospital for months and when he returned to the station he was as he is now. Pat took charge of things during his absence and later simply carried on. He'd written to Sydney explaining matters and asking for advice and information, but the charming owner – I say charming, but none of us have an inkling of what Miss A. C. S. is like – took not the slightest notice of the letters, and that made him mad."

Anne stubbed her cigarette out carefully into the ashtray and did not raise her eyes. Rusty's explanation had cleared up a great deal, but still more information was necessary before she reached the root of everything.

"Who accidentally shot the old chap?" she asked quietly, and the man fiddled with his glass and looked uncomfortable. "Was it you?"

"No, it wasn't," he cried, startled. "Does it matter?"

"I want to know."

Rusty glanced at her and sighed. "It was Pat," he answered slowly.

It was horrible, the thought of the jackaroo accidentally hitting the manager during a rabbit drive. No wonder he was so gentle and kind to the old man.

"Promise you won't tell Pat I told you?" Rusty seemed agitated. "It *was* an accident. We all saw it happen – one of the dogs knocked against Pat as he fired and the jolt spoilt his aim, the bullet ricocheted off a tree and caught Mr. Norton in the head. It was a miracle it didn't kill him. Anyway, I don't know why I've told you, or what it has to do with you."

"I'm sorry." Unthinkingly she put her hand on his arm. "It's my curiosity, and as you say, it has nothing to do with me. But it helps me to understand things better."

As they waited for the shops to reopen she was quiet and thoughtful. *Had* the jackaroo written to the solicitors when the accident happened, or had he merely pretended to do so, seeing the opportunity of taking over the reins and making something out of it for himself? Anne shook herself; the more she saw of Pat Kennedy the less she believed he would do such a thing.

The wind was beginning to blow clouds of dust across the street; it was hot and she was unusually tired. Making her way to the store to collect the groceries and wait for the jeep, she turned with the rest to a sudden squeal of brakes and distinctly heard a girlish voice cry in delight,

"Patrick Kennedy! Come and say hello!"

Anne stopped, darted into a convenient doorway and peeped through the glass window. A car as new and as smart as her own had been drawn into the side of the road, a girl as smart as Miss Carrington-Smythe had ever been was leaning excitedly through the window near the driving wheel, and Pat, with a large smile on his tanned face, was crossing the road eagerly.

The watching girl drew in her breath sharply as he bent to kiss the lovely face raised to his.

Too far away to hear their conversation, which must have been amusing, for they were both laughing, Anne watched closely. The girl could only have been about eighteen or nineteen, far too young to be interested in a man who must be well over thirty. Biting her lip, she scurried out of the doorway and ran to the stores. Rusty was waiting, perfectly sober and looking at her curiously. Anne's expression clearly informed him that her friendliness at lunchtime had quite disappeared.

When Pat joined them there was still a hint of laughter in his eyes, and he asked her quite gaily if she had bought everything she needed.

"All I had the money for," she answered, thinking of the few coppers left in her purse.

"No good going home until you've spent up," he cried genially. "I'm broke too, so let's make tracks."

The dressmaking proceeded very slowly. During the afternoons in her free time Anne struggled with the pinned material and the pattern; it looked so odd when it had been cut out and she despaired of ever putting it together.

There eventually came a time when it was tacked together and it could be tried on. The mirrors in her room were not long enough and she went into the small sitting room, which she and Pat had started to use each evening. There was a wide mirror over the fireplace and it tilted downwards, so by moving back and forward she could see the dress from neck to hem. Three times she returned to her room to make adjustments and still it was not right.

"What on earth are you doing now?" asked a voice from the doorway, and she turned round, glaring at Pat as if it was entirely his fault the dress would not fit.

"The plaguey thing wrinkles over my shoulders," she cried

with asperity. "I've unpicked it twice and still it isn't right!"

To her astonishment he crossed the room to her side, looked at the dress with his head on one side and picked up a couple of pins from the tin lid she was using.

"It needs pulling in there," she felt a pin stick in her back. "Sorry, was that you? And it needs lifting there. Does that look any better?" He turned her to the mirror again.

"How did you know what it wanted?" she asked weakly.

"I have three sisters. They always make their own clothes, and many a time I've been called upon to adjust something or pin something else."

"Three sisters?" she stared at him in amazement.

"What's wrong with that?" the laugh was in his voice now. "People do have sisters, you know. I also have a father and mother."

"How old are your sisters?" she hastened to enquire.

"The eldest is nearly forty. I'm the baby of the family." The tantalising little grin came and went quickly. "So Mother always says, anyway."

So the lovely girl leaning out of the car window and lifting her face for his kiss could not have been his sister. Perhaps she was a niece or a cousin or something.

"Oh, Miss Smith!"

"Yes, Mr. Kennedy?"

Pat turned away to light his pipe and she waited, absently fingering the material at her throat.

"Are you going to Sydney for Christmas?"

"I hadn't thought about it!" exclaimed Anne. Another three weeks and the festive season would be here again. "No, I –" she laughed rather shakily. "I shan't be going. I can't afford to!"

"Did you want to go?"

"No." Anne shook her head. "And you?"

"I'm going home, too. John always goes with me – he feels so lost, poor chap, when I'm not about. Which brings me to what

I was going to say," he puffed at his pipe, glancing at her out of the corner of his eyes. "Would you care to come with John and me? Mother told me to tell you she would be very pleased if you would."

For a moment Anne looked thunderstruck. She stared at him with wide open eyes and he returned her gaze, impassive and serious.

"B-but your mother doesn't know me," she stammered at last, and Pat shook his head.

"She knows of you."

The girl sat down abruptly and shifted her position as a pin struck into her. This sudden invitation overwhelmed her. The idea of spending a week or so with him and his parents pleased her and made her feel light-hearted.

"Well?" he asked as she hesitated.

"Thank you." Anne smiled up at him. "I would like to join you."

Pat put another match to his pipe and relaxed a little.

"Do your people live near here?" she wanted to know, thinking how little she really knew of him or his background.

"In town. Dad is retired, he had a property once on the other side of Murra Creek. Now he grows tomatoes and gets in Mother's way," he laughed, and automatically Anne smiled with him. If his father once had a property and could afford to retire, there should be little need for Pat himself to indulge in any petty pilfering.

"That's settled, then?" he asked, raising his eyebrows.

"Yes, thank you."

Pat stretched and turned to leave the room.

"Where are you going now? I was going to make some tea."

"I've some more work to do," he said wearily. "In the office."

"Couldn't I help you with the books?" she asked. "It would give you more spare time."

"You know nothing about book-keeping."

85

"I could learn."

"Not my book-keeping you couldn't," he retorted.

"Why? Is yours something special?"

"Very special," he said solemnly, watching her. "For I juggle with it. I add a little bit here and take away a little bit there until I get an answer to my satisfaction."

Over the top of the settee Anne stared at him. "But that's all wrong!" she exclaimed.

"Is it? I don't think so. Miss A. C. S. doesn't know any different, so why should I worry?"

"But, Mr. Kennedy —" her voice trailed away into silence, for she hated the idea of him doing this. It was all wrong, and if Mr. Maynard came to Gum Valley and found out what had been happening he could make things extremely awkward for the jackaroo. "Is it necessary to do this?"

"Very necessary," he answered sharply. "If I didn't juggle with the accounts we should get *nothing* at Gum Valley! As I've told you before, that woman takes every penny and gives nothing back. We need it here for replacements, depreciation — oh, for dozens of things."

"I don't like it," she murmured at length, more for something to say than anything else.

"I'm sorry."

"If — if it's found that you juggle with the accounts what will happen?" she asked, raising her eyes.

"To me?"

Anne nodded miserably. "I don't want you to go to prison."

"You have no need to worry about me," he said softly. "I'm big enough and capable enough of looking after myself. The only thing that does worry me is that if the truth were discovered about the accounts and I had to face the music, John would be alone. Rusty or Dick may have told you, I don't know, but I was the cause of this accident —

"Rusty told me," she said quietly, and he nodded.

"I thought he might have done. John doesn't remember anything about it and since then he has depended upon me for everything. If he had to go away from here it would break his heart and might send him completely mad. I feel I owe the old chap some return for what I did, even though it was an accident. If I can keep on juggling the accounts and struggle on as best we can and if neither Miss A. C. or her solicitor come up here to look round, we're all set for years. Do you understand?"

Anne gulped. This was getting out of control. She had originally come here to work, to give herself the feeling that she was being of some use to someone and she was happy as Anne Smith the cook. Having a dual personality was not at all pleasant when the other half was so disliked and was the cause of so much trouble. Mr. Maynard must be prevented from coming, she would have to write again and explain that she herself was perfectly satisfied with the way the property was being managed and would he please drop the matter altogether.

"I think I'll go to bed," she murmured huskily. "And leave you with your juggling."

"All right." Pat let go of her arm. "Goodnight, Miss Smith."

"Goodnight, Mr. Kennedy."

There were a few days of much-needed rain just before Christmas, but then it stopped and the river dropped to its normal summer level before the holidays started. Anne had gracefully refused Rusty's invitation to accompany him to Sydney, tactfully avoided Dick's questions as to what she was going to do with herself for ten days in Murra Creek.

Peter wished her a Happy Christmas and handed over a small packet before scrambling into the jeep with Alan and Dick. Rusty hung about, then he also made a presentation on behalf of himself and the others, and blushing furiously Anne stammered out her thanks. She had been totally unprepared for gifts from the men. Shouting and waving they vanished in the jeep and she went inside to see what they had given her. Peter's present was a box of dainty lace handkerchiefs and the other proved to be an expensive dressing gown of lemon-coloured silk. No wonder they had been in a hurry to be off, she thought, laughing a little as she lifted it from its nest of tissue paper. What dears they were to buy her something like this, and how she appreciated it.

Pat came in and found her standing with the dressing gown held up against her. "Do you like this?" she asked. "The dear departed have just presented me with it."

"It's very pretty." He was looking at her as he said it and quickly Anne lowered her eyes. "And if it suits you, we'll leave about half past six," he continued.

"What are we leaving in?" she asked quickly. "You were annoyed with the utility yesterday because something had gone wrong, and the men have the jeep."

"I have my own bus here," he announced casually, and the girl racked her brains to remember where she had seen a car lying about.

Mr. Norton came in with a small case and his violin, he smiled absently as he placed them on the table.

"I'm ready, Pat."

Never before had Anne taken so little time over her packing. Not that she wasn't careful, everything was placed tidily in the suitcase Pat had lent her, but it looked so pathetically empty. There was a loud honking outside the gate and after glancing round the room, she grabbed the case and rushed outside.

Pat and Mr. Norton were sitting in the front seat of a car identical with her own. It was the same model, the same colour, in fact it could have been her car. Only the number was different.

"Where did you get this?" she asked, staring hard.

"I bought it," explained Pat gravely, "in a garage."

Suspiciously she looked at him and stared again. Gone were

the rough working clothes which seemed to hang round his wiry body, in their place was a lightweight summer suit, the kind Roddie would wear, she thought wildly. He looked different altogether, a new Pat Kennedy entirely. But the voice was the same, for impatience crept into it.

"Are you going to stand there all night? Surely you've seen a car like this before?"

"Yes. But not at Gum Valley. Where has it been?"

"In the shed next to the stores. Come on, Miss Smith, we want to get away."

The thirty-two-mile journey did not seem half as long as it had done when she had last come into town in the jeep and long before they reached the outskirts of Murra Creek they could see the glow of the street lights ahead.

The car turned left into a road lined with leafy pepper trees, and she was reminded of the morning of her arrival at the station, when her first glimpse of the town had been of a pepper tree in the station yard and Pat had turned from it to come back into the waiting room. She looked up at him, he turned his head and smiled at her and after that there was no need to be nervous about anything any more.

Mr. Norton stirred and spoke for the first time.

"Here we are," there was excitement in his voice. "And there they are too." He leaned forward as the car slowed to a stop outside a large house surrounded by verandahs which were brilliantly lit. Anne had a glimpse of trees and lawns and of a group of people converging towards the gate. Ahead of them came a girl of about seven accompanied by an elderly spaniel.

"Uncle Pat!" The child dashed in front of the headlights and went to the door. "Oh, Uncle Pat, it's lovely to see you." She peered within, smiled at Mr. Norton, looked at Anne shyly and clutched her uncle's hand. "Is this your Miss Smith?"

"Yes," said Uncle Pat, smiling. "This is my Miss Smith."

"This is my mother." Pat was standing with Anne by his side as he made the introductions, and the girl held out her hand to Mrs. Kennedy. She was tall, too, a good-looking woman with snow-white hair, still graceful of figure and with a merry twinkle in her eyes.

"I'm glad you came," said Mrs. Kennedy with sincerity. "Ten days alone at Gum Valley wouldn't have been very pleasant for you, Miss Smith. Especially at Christmas."

"I'm glad you asked me to come," answered Anne simply, and turned to hold her hand to the elder Mr. Kennedy. He proved to be another tall thin wiry man, with the same dark skin and long eyelashes as his son.

In turn Anne was introduced to Pat's eldest sister and her husband, Mr. and Mrs. Ross, to Mr. and Mrs. Lang, the second sister and her husband, and to the youngest daughter of the house, Mrs. James.

"My husband is in New Guinea," she explained. "He's unable to get home this Christmas. This is my son," she brought forward a shy boy, "Teddy. And this little woman is Joy. Oh, and here's another Pat, that's Jenny's boy, and at the back – come here, Rosemary. This is the eldest of the grandchildren."

Anne looked at the lively lovely face of the girl who had hailed Pat from the car in town and gave a deep, deep sigh. She was conscious of Rosemary scrutinising her warily and guessed the girl was jealous.

The house was large and airy and comfortably furnished. In her glimpses of the rooms through the open doors they passed Anne knew that money was not scarce in this family and that Pat, with parents such as he had, would never need the extra he juggled from the accounts. Determined to forget all that and to make the most of this unexpected break in her routine, she stepped inside the room where Mrs. Kennedy was waiting.

"It's small, but I think you will be comfortable," said her hostess. "I like all the family together at Christmas, so we're a bit crowded. And I hope you don't mind the noise – the children are rarely quiet."

The girl smiled. "I'm going to enjoy myself."

This was the first Christmas she had ever spent as part of a family. Her mother, who hated cooking, usually spent the festive season in hotels and when Anne decided to have her own home she had joined with the gang in dashing from one house party to another, from one cocktail party to a dance.

The first evening was spent on the front verandah, talking lazily about everything and nothing as families do. The following morning Anne went alone to do her shopping, and before she left the house Pat called her into the lounge and held out a small bundle of notes.

"This is your bonus," he explained. "Your share of the sale of fruit." Anne looked down at the money and quickly into his face. "Don't you remember? Rusty took the cases to the station the day you came into town. I gave the men theirs before they left."

Anne hesitated, smiled and took it with a word of thanks. Now she was going to spend it, principally on gifts for her host, hostess and the children, but in view of this unexpected windfall she could now afford to buy something for herself. She wandered round the town, there was no one she knew to stop and talk to her so she had plenty of time to make her purchases.

Throughout the rest of the day, during the last-minute preparations, she was conscious all the time of the Kennedy family watching her and appraising her. There was a slight air of restraint, anyone with less self-possession than Anne might have felt at a loss and ill at ease, she had travelled the world over and was used to the behaviour of strangers. These people were strangers, there was only Pat and Mr. Norton she knew.

It was Joy, the little girl, who explained the restraint. Anne had offered to assist in the kitchen during the preparations for the evening meal and had been shooed out by Mrs. Lang.

"Go talk to Dad," she advised. "There are three women in here already, Miss Smith, and that's two too many! Get him to show you his tomatoes – if you show an interest there you'll be his friend for life!"

So Anne searched the garden for Mr. Kennedy, but he had wandered off somewhere else in the company of his son, sons-in-law and Mr. Norton, and the lovely spacious garden was deserted. She admired the shrubs and the trees, paused by the beds of asters, zinnias and late gladioli, and came to a stop on a garden seat set invitingly beneath a huge wattle tree. It was there Joy found her and she came daintily across the lawn and sat down.

"Are you hot?" she asked politely, and Anne shook her head.

"Not when I'm out of the direct sun, It's very shady and cool just here."

"Yes, Grandpa loves his garden," said the child, swinging her legs. "There's a nice garden at Gum Valley, isn't there?"

"A beautiful one," agreed the girl. "Have you been there often?"

"Oh, lots of times. Granny sometimes drives out to see Uncle Pat, but not in the summer because the dust makes her sneeze. It's such a dusty road, isn't it? Uncle Pat takes me out during the school holidays and last year I stayed for a week." She looked troubled. "But he hasn't mentioned me going this time."

"He's been very busy lately, but perhaps if you remind him he'll suggest it." Anne looked down at the fair head with its long shining hair. "I'd like you to come, then I should have someone to talk to."

"Oh!" Joy's face lit up with delight. "Do you mean that? I'd love to, we must ask Uncle, I think he'll say yes. Thank you, Miss Smith." She put her hand gently on the other's arm. "Are you going to marry Uncle Pat?"

"Whatever put that idea into your head?" asked Anne, startled.

"Well, yesterday, before you came, Granny and Mummy were talking about you and Granny said it was strange that Uncle Pat was bringing you here for Christmas as he'd never brought a young lady home before. Mummy laughed and said perhaps he was going to marry you." Joy drew back, the better to look at the girl's flushed face. "I think it would be nice," she announced solemnly. "Wouldn't you like to marry Uncle Pat?"

"Yes," said Anne thoughtfully, "I would." She recollected herself quickly. "But you mustn't *ever* tell him or anyone else that I said so! It must be a great secret between us."

The child's eyes glowed. "A lovely secret! I shan't tell anyone and I can keep secrets ever so well."

Anne put her arm round the child's shoulders, turning over in her mind the idea of being married to the jackaroo. It sounded strange, no one she knew had ever done such a thing, but it must happen, then they had little jackaroos who grew up to be over six feet tall and who had cool grey eyes which would suddenly twinkle with laughter.

"Dreaming, Miss Smith?" asked a voice behind her, and she spun round on the seat.

"How long have you been there?" she wanted to know.

"I've just arrived. Why?"

"Oh, nothing," she answered casually, aware of Joy giving her a glance of conspiracy.

"Joy, Grandpa has brought home something special and if you want your share – no need to say any more," he remarked as the child leapt up and ran across the lawn. Sitting down in the seat she had vacated he looked at Anne quizzically. "Is it the heat that has made you flushed, or is there another reason for the colour in your face, Miss Smith?"

"The heat, I think, Mr. Kennedy."

"It's no hotter here than at Gum Valley."

Anne met his smiling glance and laughed. No wonder his family had been appraising her, they were wondering what was to be the outcome of the friendship between the only son of their house and the cook at Gum Valley. In that respect, she reminded herself proudly, my birth is as good as his, and her face lost its colour as she remembered who she was. How could she ever tell him she was the owner of Gum Valley? She imagined her halting explanation and could visualise the changing expressions on his face and could almost hear the torrent of abuse which would fall upon her. Anne shuddered and thankfully looked up when she heard someone coming from the house. Mr. Kennedy and Rosemary came towards them, the latter carrying a basket.

"Granny wants some lemons picking, also some tomatoes and lettuce," she announced. "Will you come with me, Pat?"

"Must I? It's so hot in the orchard," her uncle complained, and his father smiled and Anne saw the frown of anger crease the girl's wide forehead.

"I'll come if I may," Anne cried, jumping to her feet.

"In that case, we'll all go," said Pat, stretching lazily and pretending not to notice the reproachful glance Anne flung in his direction. Standing by the lemon tree, Rosemary looked at the older girl.

"I'm sure I've seen you somewhere before," she said slowly.

"I don't think so!" exclaimed Anne quickly. "Unless it was in town. I did come in one day recently."

"It wasn't then," stated Rosemary flatly. "It was in Sydney, I'm convinced it was."

"Perhaps it was someone else who looked like me," suggested Anne.

"Where did you live?"

Miss Smith hesitated. "I was working in a flat at Rose Bay." That was the truth, she *had* worked in her own home.

"No, it couldn't have been there," said the younger girl thoughtfully. "It may have been at Terrigal or Palm Beach."

Anne was silent, aware of the two men watching her. Rosemary shrugged her shoulders impatiently, as though the tantalising memory which eluded her would return at some later date, and turned to pick the lemons.

The heat of the day did not change much even after the sun had set, the children were sent to bed early and the adults began to decorate the Christmas tree and bring forth their presents. As unobtrusively as she could Anne hung her few gifts on the tree, there was one each for Mr. and Mrs. Kennedy, one for each of the children and a small oblong box for Pat. Also a parcel for Mr. Norton. The verandahs were then decorated with coloured streamers and fairy lights and after that they all sat on the lawn until nearly midnight, convinced they would not sleep if they did go to bed. But one by one, yawning loudly, they departed knowing that they would be awakened early by the excited girl and boys. Mrs. Kennedy was finally left sitting with her son. He glanced at his watch and looked at her.

"Happy Christmas, Mother."

"Is it past midnight already? Happy Christmas to you, too, son."

She watched him fill his pipe and looked at his face in the light of the match.

"How are things out there, Pat?"

"Rotten," he answered bluntly, and because he knew his mother would understand what he was talking about, because she had lived on the land for years and because he wanted to talk and he knew she wanted to listen, he described his difficulties at Gum Valley. She frowned as his voice died away.

"I can't understand it. According to your reckoning, despite the fact that you've had to alter the accounts, Gum Valley has made an excellent profit during the past twelve months?" He nodded in confirmation. "You've written to the solicitor and explained it all and still they won't grant you any more for working expenses."

"Not a penny."

"It seems odd to me, son."

Pat leaned forward. "It's more than odd. All I can think of is that woman has such expensive tastes she won't allow her income to drop at all. If she would only realise that by spending money on modern machinery and other labour-saving devices she would get an even better return. I don't know why I bother," he added moodily. "I certainly don't get any thanks for what I've done, and if Mr. Maynard ever did come out here and go through the books I'd get it in the neck!"

"I don't like the thought of you juggling with those accounts," said his mother. "For I doubt if you could prove that the difference had been spent on the station."

"All the men know what I'm doing."

"They would back you up, yes, I know that. But the fact remains you do the accounts and John signs whatever you tell him to sign. He's still the manager, even if he is a bit –" she hesitated. "Well, peculiar, shall I say."

"Poor John." Pat put another match to his pipe. "It's no use discussing anything with him, he'll listen and then say, 'Do whatever you think best.' I wonder if I went to Sydney and had it out with Miss A. C. S., if that would do any good?"

"It might," agreed Mrs. Kennedy. "Providing you didn't let your dislike of her and your temper get the better of you."

He smiled across at her in the subdued light and she decided, while he was in this mellow confiding mood, to ask a question which had been trembling on her tongue for quite a while.

"Pat, who is Miss Smith?"

"Officially the cook. Unofficially," he frowned, "I don't know. She's been very well educated and speaks French and German fluently, which pleases Jan. She's well spoken and wears her clothes with an air, as though she has been used to better things than she possesses now, if you know what I mean. Also, she wasn't a cook and had never been one."

"So you don't get properly fed?"

"We do now." His little grin came and went quickly. "I told her she would have to go if she didn't give us respectable meals. I discovered she had been searching for the old lady's cookery books and since then there have been no complaints. Sometimes, quite unconsciously, she gives orders as though she's been accustomed to maids, butlers and what else have you, and she handles Rusty in the manner of a lady born."

"How does she handle you, son?"

"Oh, I'm just the jackaroo and I'm treated as such."

Are you? wondered his mother. "So you know nothing of her background?"

"Nothing," he agreed, and stood up. "I think it's time we went in, young Joy will be dancing on my bed about five in the morning and the house will resound to the noise of childish mirth because it's Christmas Day."

"You'll be as noisy as anyone, yet you're not a child." she cried affectionately. "How old are you now? Thirty-one?"

"Thirty-two," he answered with a grimace, and bent to give her a goodnight kiss.

The children slept until six, then the noise started. Anne was awakened by tin trumpets outside the bedroom door and wearing the silk dressing gown presented by the men, she went out to join the fun. The tree was stripped and Anne did not feel out of anything when she discovered four parcels on her knee. The first she opened was from Mr. Norton. Anne stared as the wrappings parted and disclosed a cookery book.

"Pat once said you needed one," explained the manager, looking at her anxiously. "I remembered, you see."

"It's what I want — what I need," cried Anne in a trembling voice, not daring to look across the room to where Pat was standing. "Thank you very much, Mr. Norton." Acting on an impulse she kissed his cheek and he smiled with delighted surprise.

The box from her host and hostess contained good quality stationery, the sort of gift they would present to anyone staying beneath their roof just to show they were not forgotten. The third was shown as from "The Girls" – Anne presumed the girls were the three sisters – and proved to be a small white handbag. Aware that they were now all watching, she opened the box from Pat and with a flush on her cheeks she held up a dainty silver chain from which hung the most exquisite cameo she had ever seen. Accustomed as she was to expensive presents, Anne knew this was no cheap trinket, and with shining eyes she turned to thank him.

"Aren't you going to kiss him too?" asked Joy impishly, and Anne's composure vanished.

"Later," said Pat, coming to the rescue. "Certainly not when all you folk are standing staring!"

There was a laugh in which all but Rosemary joined, and her mother looked at her with exasperation in her eyes.

"Now all this excitement is over," said Mr. Kennedy a few minutes later when the three children had gone to play with their new toys, "may I make a suggestion?"

"Certainly, dear," cried his wife.

He squinted up at the blue sky. "It's going to be even hotter than it was yesterday, so I suggest we take a picnic lunch on the river bank and spend the day swimming."

"An excellent idea," agreed his eldest daughter. "We'd planned dinner for tonight as it will be cooler then and even Joy is old enough to stay up. Don't you all agree?"

About midday the three cars came to a standstill on the river bank, and hampers, folding chairs and cases of soft drinks were unloaded from the boots. The cases were immediately carried into the water and left in a shady place where they would stay cool and after some argument as to the best place to sit, rugs were spread out, chairs unfolded and one by one they disappeared behind trees to change into swimsuits. Within fifteen minutes of their arrival, all of them, including Mr. and Mrs. Kennedy, were in the water.

After a cup of tea about four o'clock, Anne went to the bushes to change. Pausing by Pat's car, she smiled at the sight of Mr. Norton sleeping peacefully on the back seat and started to comb her hair, using the driving mirror for her reflection. Her throat was sunburnt and as she looked at it she put out her hand for her bag and withdrew Pat's necklace. The silver chain ran through her fingers and she fingered the cameo gently, thinking that he still had to be thanked for it.

Whistling, Pat came towards her, his towel swinging from one hand, and swiftly she thrust the cameo back into her handbag. He looked more tanned than ever in the white silk shirt and his hair was wet and untidy.

"John still asleep?" he peered into the car.

They both looked compassionately at the placid face of the manager and Anne drew away.

"Shall we have a walk?" asked Pat quickly.

She nodded and in silence they started along the bank.

Scrambling over rocks and fallen trees they turned with the bank, each twist of the river brought another view of placid water, sunlight and cool shadows. Everything was still and quiet, only the birds were lively and awake in the heat of the afternoon.

Suddenly there seemed to be nothing to say. They climbed the bank in silence when they could no longer walk along the water's edge and started down again after they had passed the obstruction, Pat held out his hand to help her leap the tufts of thick grass and side by side they jumped the last two feet. The water here was very shallow and chuckled loudly as it passed over the smooth stones and pebbles, rippling like gold where the sunlight caught it.

"It's a beautiful river," Anne murmured.

"At the moment," he agreed, and pointed to a tree high on the opposite bank. "See the mark on the trunk? The water reached up there during the floods."

"It's almost unbelievable."

"There are a lot of things that are unbelievable," he answered slowly, tightening his grip on her wrist and turning her to face him.

"Such as?" she asked smiling.

"Such as a confirmed bachelor and woman-hater like myself wanting to kiss you," he said, and swept her into his arms.

CHAPTER SIX

A PARTY HAD been arranged for the following evening and Anne insisted on helping with the preparations. So Mrs. Kennedy drew her into the kitchen and placed before her a miscellaneous collection of fruit, with the request that it be prepared for fruit salads and drinks. Armed with a sharp knife Anne sat down and as she peeled and sliced and chopped she began to think over what had happened to her during the past twelve months. The memory of the few minutes in Pat's arms the previous afternoon brought a sudden flush to her face. It had been more wonderful than she had ever imagined it could be and banished forever any doubts as for her love for him. Encircled by his strong brown arms and with his face resting against hers, she had clung to him, unable to speak with emotion, and they had stood close together on the water's edge until someone had come sliding down the bank and a childish voice had cried,

"Uncle Pat, we're going home now!"

That had been the end of their privacy during the afternoon. Pat had muttered something beneath his breath and had given her hand a last hard squeeze and silently the three of them had retreated their steps and rejoined the others. Since then they had not been alone, they had behaved towards each other exactly as they had always done before, or so they thought, but Mrs. Kennedy had not been deceived by their casual attitude. Something had happened, she knew, for she loved her only son deeply and he could not altogether mislead her with his easy air. She had noticed a new softness in his eyes whenever he glanced at the girl. To the best of her recollection he had never looked at anyone as he did at Miss Anne Smith. As the little jobs in the kitchen were completed she sat down opposite Anne to help with the fruit.

"I think fruit and salads are the best possible things you can eat this weather," she said, and the girl nodded. "How do you manage at the station for vegetables?"

"We've plenty," Anne smiled. "They're always so fresh and succulent – we're not short of water, so perhaps that's one reason."

Mrs. Kennedy looked up from her task. "A lot different from Sydney," she remarked. "Where did you live, Miss Smith? Anywhere with a garden?"

"No, there are no such things as gardens when you live in a flat.. I was at Rose Bay for a long time, with lovely views of the Harbour from my window."

"Gum Valley will certainly be a change after that!"

"It is, but I like it. Very much. I'm very happy there."

"It's a pleasant place." Mrs. Kennedy frowned. "A great pity the owner won't be bothered about it."

Anne lowered her eyes and concentrated on slicing peaches into thin wafers, willing the other woman to change the conversation and not bring Miss Carrington-Smythe into it. She had a horror of the truth coming to light during the time she was staying under the roof of these pleasant people; it would be far better to tell Pat everything when she was alone with him in the homestead. His anger would be easier to bear if she was the only one to witness it; she was ashamed of her duplicity and not for the first time wished she had not entered so gaily into the role of the cook. Pat had not told her he loved her, but she knew he did, she had seen it in his eyes and had heard it in the caressing tone of his voice as he whispered her name over and over again, and she was content to wait. Later she would have to trust to the depth of his affection to forgive her.

"And your parents? Do you live with them?" Mrs. Kennedy interrupted her thoughts.

"My father died many years ago, and my mother," the affectionate smile which always accompanied the thought of her mother softened Anne's face, "she can't stay in one place for any length of time. At the moment she's in Papeete —" she stopped in confusion, and as if in answer to her silent prayer Pat came into the kitchen and raised his eyebrows at the sight of their energy.

"I see you're busy, Miss Smith."

"Need you be so formal?" asked his mother.

"We were never properly introduced," he said solemnly.

"In that case I'll make the introductions myself. Anne, may I present my son Patrick?" It was a beautiful gesture on her part and she did not miss the grateful glance Pat gave her as she shook Anne's hand.

"I'm more than pleased to make your acquaintance, Anne."

"Thank you, Patrick."

The three of them started to laugh and Rosemary, passing the window, wished she could remember where she had seen Miss Smith before.

The party was a success despite the excessive heat, and Anne thoroughly enjoyed herself, in fact she enjoyed every hour of her stay with the Kennedys until Pat fetched Gum Valley's mail from the Post Office one morning and handed her an envelope. She knew immediately that it had been sent by Mr. Maynard and a sudden premonition seized her as she slit the envelope. The letter was in reply to her own and was brief; it stated curtly that it was quite evident that Miss Smith was allowing the man Kennedy to play upon her inexperience as regards station matters and that he, as her solicitor, had no intention of letting the matter drop until it had been thoroughly investigated. Thereupon he proposed to come out West at a date to be arranged and would find out for himself just how far things had gone.

Anne caught her breath and crushed the letter in her hand. She did not want Mr. Maynard up here. No explanations were necessary, for the fault was entirely her own and she, at least, understood the position in which Pat had been placed.

In her bedroom she frantically wrote a reply, ordering him to stay where he was and not to come to Gum Valley under any circumstances. "I can handle this matter myself," she wrote, "and I don't want any interference."

Unfortunately when Mr. Maynard read that he immediately began to think Miss Smith had written it under pressure and made plans to leave Sydney at the beginning of the New Year.

Anne went alone into the garden that evening. Sitting on the seat beneath the wattle tree she fanned herself with her handkerchief and wished they were back at Gum Valley; she had an idea that the solicitor was too conscientious to take much notice of her letter and she wanted to prepare Pat in case the old man did arrive complete with his briefcase and his most forbidding expression.

A hand moved near her throat and tilted back her chin. Pat's dark face bent over hers and her hand went up to touch his. He kissed her gently and sat down, his arm tight around her shoulders.

"Do you know," he said quietly, looking at her, "I have a feeling you love me."

"Have you now?" Anne looked surprised. "I wonder what gave you that impression?"

He went on looking at her, at the glossy hair and sparkling brown eyes, at the tanned skin showing at her throat, and caught his breath.

"Do you, Anne?" he asked urgently. "Do you?"

"Yes."

As direct and truthful as always, he thought, tightening his arm and drawing her closer.

"Isn't that strange?" he murmured. "I love you too."

"Oh, Pat, that's what I've been wanting you to say," she cried with a little sob and gasped as he crushed her against him.

"You're squeezing me," she managed to gasp out, and he slackened his hold.

"Don't you like it?" he asked, smiling.

"Yes," she confessed with a soft laugh. "But – darling – not quite – so hard!"

"Say that again," he demanded.

"What?"

"Darling."

Anne turned so that she could put her hands up to his face and drew it down again to hers. "Darling. *Darling!*"

"This isn't like you," she murmured at length. "You've never spoken to me like this before. Always you've been impatient, curt –"

"My sweet, how could I be otherwise – at Gum Valley? Use your common sense!" She laughed softly. "What else could I do before the men? Had you forgotten that only you and I shared that big house, that we were alone night after night? I had to be careful, sweet. I couldn't have your name discussed lightly by such as Rusty."

"I hadn't thought of that," she admitted.

"No, I don't think you had. It was so hard at times too, for

I desperately wanted to kiss you, especially when you flew into a rage with me. But I promise I'll never speak to you like that again."

"Never?"

"Never. Please believe me."

Anne looked wise. "Not even if I move your pipe or disturb any of your other belongings?"

Pat laughed softly and kissed her again before replying. "Perhaps I'd better not promise after all, for I'm only human, Anne," he lowered his voice a little. "When I've straightened everything up at Gum Valley I'm going to talk to you like this again, only more seriously. Until then, will you just go on loving me and be content to wait?"

She bit her lip, knowing quite well what he meant. Until he had had things out with either the solicitor or Miss Carrington-Smythe he was not going to ask her to marry him and she nodded dumbly, wishing, not for the first time, that she had been born plain Anne Smith with little or no money.

It was raining hard when Anne awakened the following morning, and she went into breakfast to find a discussion in progress. Pat gave her a smiling glance.

"It's rained all night and the weather forecast says continuing bad weather all over the State, so I think, if it's agreeable to you, we'll go back this morning. Do you mind leaving so soon, Anne?"

"Not at all."

"I must be there when the men return and if the river does rise a little, as it probably will, there will be a few things needing attention. This arrangement all right with you, John?"

"Yes, Pat." Mr. Norton nodded his head.

The four of them — Joy was with them, for her promised visit to Gum Valley — left the township about half past ten and they had not gone far along the road before Anne realised this was not going to be a very comfortable journey. As they were leaving, Mr. Kennedy had placed old sacks and a spade in the boot of the car and they were going to be needed, for already the back wheels were sliding gently on the muddy surface, as if they were developing minds of their own and were desirous of going in a different direction. Pat drove with a frown on his face, his hands gripping the wheel hard as he corrected each skid. The track sloped sharply on either side into what was known as the table drain and once the back wheels slid down there he knew it would be almost impossible to get the car back on to the crown of the road.

Ahead was the creek and as he crossed the wooden bridge Pat glanced down. Water was flowing high and fast towards the river, after another day's rain such as this it would reach the wooden decking and then slowly cover it as dirty muddy water spread out on either side, and their only means of entry into town would be cut off. The weight of the big car made the flimsy bridge rattle menacingly and it needed just that gentle movement of the structure to loosen from its position, where it had risen slowly with the water, the case which had fallen from the utility months before and which had lain unnoticed in the dry bed of the creek. It bobbed on the water and as its owner disappeared into the rain, moved slowly with the current along with a large amount of dead brushwood towards the rising river.

Joy glanced back through the dirt-streaked windows. "The creek is right up, Uncle Pat. If it crosses the bridge we shan't be able to get into town and I shan't have to go to school!"

The rest of the journey was painfully slow and the car proceeded the whole way in second gear, but fortunately it was uneventful and when they drew up thankfully at Gum Valley the rain was still coming from above. "As though someone is standing there with a bucket!" as Joy described it. Jan, wearing an old raincoat over his shoulders, came towards them and after welcoming their safe arrival announced that he had the kettle boiling and a meal ready. Anne could have hugged him for that information.

"Think it would be advisable to ring the store and ask them to send out more groceries when Rusty leaves town?" she asked as she sat in the kitchen.

Pat nodded, thinking of the state of the road when Rusty and the others returned in the jeep. That should be able to get through with little difficulty, providing the creek had not overflowed its banks.

"The forecast later this morning was for more rain," volunteered Jan, glancing at each in turn. "And warnings of local floodings in the upper reaches of the river."

Something pleasant had happened to those two during the Christmas holidays, he thought. Pat's grey eyes were tender whenever they met the girl's clear glance, and she moved round the kitchen about her accustomed tasks with a light joyful step.

In the late afternoon Anne stood on the verandah of the homestead and gazed out across the paddock towards the river, which was unseen behind the curtain of rain. Pat had reported there was no rise as yet, but a great deal depended upon how much rain had fallen further back. The clouds seemed low enough to almost touch the tree-tops, they scurried across the heavens as though it was imperative they should unburden themselves before travelling elsewhere.

A few flowers had been picked from near the verandah and after she had rinsed off the mud under a tap Anne left them to dry a little. Joy was curled up on the settee with her dolls and was half asleep; she said drowsily that as soon as she had had tea she would go to bed.

As she washed her, combed her hair and tucked her up in the little bed placed beside her own in the large bedroom, Anne wondered what it would feel like if she had to do these pleasant little tasks every night. The thought brought a delicate colour to her face and as she bent to kiss Joy, the child asked sleepily,

"Has Uncle Pat asked you to marry him yet?"

"No, dear."

"I hope he does. Ask him to say goodnight, too, will you?"

Anne crossed to the door and called, Pat came down the hall, his pipe in his hand, and looked at her enquiringly.

"Joy wants you to kiss her goodnight."

"I hope Anne has the same idea in mind," he murmured as together they went into the bedroom. Joy smiled, more asleep than awake, said goodnight and closed her eyes. Outside the door Pat looked thoughtful.

"So during the next few days we're to pretend she's ours?" he asked, and she nodded, her eyes dancing. "Do you know, sweet, I rather like the idea!"

"Oh, Pat!" she laughed as he kissed her, and slipping his arm round her waist he ran her through the house on to the verandah. But at the sound of the drumming rain on the iron roof his expression changed.

"Anne, the river has started to rise," he announced quietly.

The rain had ceased the following morning, but the air was heavy and humid, and Jan, who was quite a weather prophet, said it had not finished. Storms were to be expected, and the wireless reports bore out his statements. The river had risen an odd foot or so during the night and they knew there was more rise to be expected, but none of them anticipated a flood.

"It will probably be a banker," said Pat as they walked from the bank across the wet paddock about nine o'clock. He turned to gaze back at the river. "It's that bluff that worries me," Anne glanced at him inquiringly and he pointed with his finger. "See those four trees in the protruding piece of land? One of them had nearly all the soil washed from its roots during the last rise in the river, the current swings round by the bank there and if there's much more the tree may go and loosen the ground where the others are standing. Once the trees fall and the ground is softened and made loose the river will make its way through and over the bluff, then there'll be nothing to stop it coming across this paddock and so into the garden of the house."

Anne could see he was worried; he kept glancing at the sky and around the horizon, where black clouds moved in a solemn procession.

"I'll be glad when the men get back," he muttered. "It might be as well to let the fences down and move the sheep away from the bank on to higher ground. And Jan, I think we'll bring a milker into the garden, with Joy here we mustn't be without milk, and also a couple of sheep, they can be kept near the store shed. We'll need meat."

Pat was making his preparations well ahead and as the girl walked beside him over the soggy ground she realised that Gum Valley would never go downhill with such a man in charge. He had foresight and knew what he wanted, as far as the station work was concerned he was rarely wrong.

Rusty, Dick, Alan and Peter arrived back just before midday, reporting a horrible journey. The creek was full, they explained, and another half-inch of rain over the area would see it over-flowing and the road cut in two. They were hungry and did full justice to the very generous meal Anne placed before them. All of them were surprised to see Joy and after dinner Rusty lingered in the kitchen and waited until the others had departed.

"Why did she come out?" he asked, jerking his thumb in the direction the little girl had taken.

Anne looked surprised. "She came with her uncle for the school holidays."

"Bad time to bring a child out here," he said. "Has Pat gone mad? If the river floods she'll be stuck here."

"So will we all," answered Anne, clearing the table. "I'm looking after her, and she's little trouble, in fact everything is a great adventure!"

He looked at her closely. "What have you been doing with yourself in Murra Creek during the holidays?"

"This and that," she said airily, shaking soap powder into the sink.

"See anything of Pat while you were there?"

"Naturally, seeing he was in town."

"Been out with him?"

"Why are you looking at me like that?"

Rusty grabbed her arm. "You didn't answer my question, Anne. Did you go out with Pat?"

"I can't see why my actions have anything to do with you," said Anne coldly.

"They've a lot to do with me!" he cried roughly. "I've been thinking of you the whole time I was away, I couldn't get you out of my mind. You've no idea how I've been looking forward to getting back –"

"Let me go!" she said quietly.

"Anne –"

"*Rusty!*" Pat was standing in the doorway, his face flushed a deep red. "Take your hands off Miss Smith. *Immediately!*"

"Is she your property?" asked the groom insultingly, and moved hastily across the kitchen as Pat moved slowly towards him. "All right, Pat, let it go."

He had had a taste before of the jackaroo's fist when Pat had lost his temper, and Rusty remembered it with an inward shudder. He was no coward and could hold his own, in fact he had done so in many a drunken brawl, but there was something unnerving in Pat's hot-headed eloquence and clenched fists. Without a word he left the kitchen.

Aware of Anne standing near him as if to warn him to be

careful, Pat kept his hands by his side with a great effort. It would not do to have friction between them when there was so much on hand, when they might all be in danger from the muddy waters of the river. This was what he had been afraid of since the very beginning – the one lonely woman as a disturbing faction among the many lonely men.

Early the following morning the radio was blaring loudly, and as she prepared breakfast in the dull light of another day Anne listened to the reports of the rainfall further back and to the readings of the river. It was rising rapidly at Bathurst and Wellington and was being swollen by tributaries on either bank, if the rain continued in the watersheds a major flood would follow. Already people were being advised to leave their homes on the low-lying banks and seek shelter on higher ground, farmers were warned to move their flocks and a note of sympathy could be heard in the announcer's voice as he read further news from along the hundreds of miles of river banks.

"We're for it," cried Dick fatalistically. "It's risen another two or three feet here during the night, and there's all that water still to come from further back. Hope you have plenty of grub in, Anne!"

As he spoke Alan, with mud up to his knees, came in with the vegetables and placed them on the table.

"If the river comes over there won't be no more," he announced gloomily. "Unless Pat finds time from letting down his blessed fences to put up a what-you-may-call-it wall."

"A retainer wall?" asked Anne, hazarding a guess.

"That's right. If the bluff goes and the water sweeps across the paddock there, my garden's had it!"

He went out muttering something beneath his breath, and when Pat came into the kitchen a little while later Anne mentioned what the old gardener had said.

"All in good time," he cried impatiently. "I can't be everywhere at once."

"You're tired and worried, darling, aren't you?" She glanced quickly round the kitchen. Joy had followed Alan into the muddy garden and they were alone, so she put her arms round his neck and hugged him close to her. "Will it help if I tell you again how I love you?"

"It will help a lot," he answered smiling, and kissed her, forgetting for a few moments the rain and the wind and the work that had still to be done outside.

"You're awfully bristly," remarked Anne a little while later.

"I'm sorry, but there wasn't time to do anything about it this morning. Do you mind very much?"

She shook her head. "Bristles or not, you're still my Pat."

"Always," he promised.

Whistling, more at peace with the world and the turbulent river, he squelched his way down the track towards the shearing shed. It had leaked badly last time it had rained, he would just glance at it now and then ride out to the men who were four miles away on the fences. The noise of a truck changing gear made him pause and turn, looking down the track to the ramp; a dark blue utility came into sight from behind the trees, sliding a little from one side to the other. Pat went towards it, wondering who had ventured out to Gum Valley on such a day. The utility stopped and a cheerful face looked out of the open window.

"Howdy, Pat!"

"What brings you here?" asked the jackaroo, very surprised. The driver of the utility lived twelve miles nearer town and his property would escape any floodwaters which might cover the road.

"A suitcase." With both hands he lifted something gingerly from the seat beside him. "I guess it belongs to your cook. Easy with it, Pat, one end is loose and is falling apart."

Pat took hold of the wet fibre suitcase and stared at it in astonishment. "Wherever did you find it?"

"It was washed into a backwater along with some logs and brushwood, one of the men found and brought it in. My missus was insistent that I brought it out while the road was still clear, she said the young lady would be glad of what's inside."

"Miss Smith will be very pleased to get it, even if its contents are a trifle wet and muddy. Thanks a lot for bringing it out, Jack." He laughed, imagining Anne's delight when he handed her the case.

The other man looked at him oddly. "Oh, and here's some butter, you might need it before long." He handed over another heavy parcel. "By the way, I passed a year-one car 'way back, it was heading in this direction, struggling gamely through the mud, and the owner, a woman, assured me that she didn't want assistance and was quite all right. Expecting any visitors?"

"In this weather?" Pat glanced up at the sky again, the clouds were darkening and a chill wind was blowing across the river. "No one is coming that I know of."

"Just thought I'd warn you. She must be coming here, for there's no one at home at Riverview – so if she doesn't turn up you'd better go out and look for the body."

"Damn that for a tale," retorted Pat. "I've plenty on my plate as it is." He waved towards the river. "What do you think of it, Jack?"

"It's coming all right," said the other sombrely. "And it's going to be a big one."

"As bad as it was a couple of years ago?"

"Or worse." He started the engine. "I'll be getting back. Hope everything goes all right with you all out here. If the telephone wires come down I suppose they'll send out the little plane looking for distress signals," he grinned. "Don't let anyone break their necks during the next few days, will you?"

Pat frowned. If anyone did have an accident and the water was over the road, heaven alone knew what would happen.

Anne's suitcase, after lying on the dry bed of the creek for

months and then soaked in the river for days, was on its last
legs. As Pat picked it up one sodden end dropped with a dull
"plop" on to the ground and a few pieces of lingerie followed it.
Smiling as he bent to pick them up, he stuffed them in the open
end and with the box of butter under the other arm moved towards the house. But as he reached the verandah steps the case
seemed to disintegrate under his arm and all the contents slipped to the wooden boards. The butter was placed on a chair and
Pat knelt to gather together the wet clothes, and as he did so
his fingers closed on Anne's passport.

Curiously he held it up, wondering why Miss Smith had
packed this into her case, for it could not be hers. But the photograph, unlike most passport photos, was a good one and un-
deniably Anne. He stared hard at the words beneath it, "Anne
Carrington-Smythe", and sat down abruptly beside the broken
fibre case. Hardly able to credit the evidence of his eyes, he
flicked over the pages quickly. All the personal particulars tal-
lied with the girl he knew, and it was more than evident that
the passport had been well used; visas had been stamped upon
it for most of the European countries, for Egypt, India, Canada
and the U.S.A.

Pat picked up the odd piece of paper and though the writing
was blurred and the edges were stuck over towards the centre
it was not undecipherable. This told him bluntly that Miss
Carrington-Smythe possessed the capabilities of an air pilot,
and as a wave of savage fury swept through him he rumpled the
paper into a ball and flung it across the wet lawn. Dully he
gazed at the pile of clothing. It wasn't possible that Anne, *his*
Anne, the only girl he had ever loved, should be, in reality, the
owner of Gum Valley and the mysterious woman he had hated
for so long. It didn't make sense. What was she doing here cooking for seven men in an out-of-date kitchen when she had all
that money? Unless – his eyes narrowed. Unless Miss Carrington-Smythe had come here on purpose to find out what was

happening on the property and by so doing had made such a fool of him that he would never forgive her. He remembered, too, her curiosity about the small office and the way he did the accounts, the way she avoided any discussion about where she had been living previously and her reticence about her past life.

It was raining heavily again and in one quick movement Pat gathered up everything from the verandah and went into the house. The case and the clothing was flung on to the small table in the sitting room and with a scowl on his dark face he stared out of the window towards the river. The coming flood was forgotten for the moment, bitter anger gripped him, and catching sight of Alan in the garden he shouted harshly,

"Tell that cook to come here!"

Alan raised his head, met the cold grey eyes and turned to do his bidding. Ten minutes later, when his patience was well-nigh exhausted, Pat heard Anne's light footsteps in the hall.

"I'm sorry to be so long, dear," she said as she came in. "But I had to – why –" she stopped near the table, glanced uncertaintly at what had been thrown upon it and looked quickly into his face. "My case!"

"Yes, your case, Miss Carrington-Smythe," he said icily, and she gave a little cry.

"Pat!"

For a long moment they stared at each other across the table and Anne was the first to lower her eyes. Her heart was pounding and her throat felt dry. She was shocked into speechlessness and continued to stand before him, her face flushing guiltily. It was not difficult to guess what he was thinking and she was unprepared, for the truth had come unexpectedly and altogether in the wrong way.

"So it *is* true?" he asked between his teeth.

"Yes. But I can explain –" she faltered.

"Your explanation had better be a good one." His face had not altered its expression and his eyes were half closed; the hard glint in them made the girl shudder. He drew a deep breath, but before he could speak she was by his side, her hand on his arm.

"Pat, listen to me," she pleaded quickly. "I was going to tell you –"

He shook himself free of her grip. "Why did you come here as Anne Smith, the cook ?"

"I'll tell you and you must believe me. I came because I was so tired of Sydney and the life I was leading, I wanted a complete change. It suddenly became futile, the dashing here and there and never getting anywhere, I was tired of my friends, tired of everything. I wanted to work for my living, to get some satisfaction out of *doing* something, and I wanted to live where it was quiet and peaceful." She hesitated, stole another glance at his angry face and went on sturdily : "Then I remembered I had a property out West –"

"How kind of you to remember it at all," he sneered.

"Stop that ! Oh, yes, the fault was mine, I admit it, and I've regretted ever since I came here that I didn't know much about it before. Until then I know I hadn't given Gum Valley much thought –"

"No thought," he corrected her. "No thought at all, judging by the way you refused to answer letters and left everything in the hands of your solicitor. You were too busy being a social butterfly to give any thought to the place where your money was coming from."

"Have it your own way." She stopped and swallowed hard. "I went to Mr. Maynard and asked – asked him to tell me about it. Its very position, so far from anywhere, made it attractive, that was what I wanted so much. He told me he had been receiving letters from you asking for the services of a cook –"

"And while you were there I presume he also told you that

Gum Valley was not a paying proposition and suggested to you that it would be a good opportunity to find out why?"

"Yes," she admitted truthfully, twisting her hands together and wondering helplessly if her explanations would melt the icy look in his eyes.

"And I also presume you wrote to him after your arrival here and said that from your observations the station seemed to be quite prosperous, that the manager was incapable of acting as such and that the whole concern was being managed by a jackaroo?"

"Yes." It was no use denying it, for that was precisely what she had done.

"And I suppose he replied saying you must find out more of what was happening?" he continued ruthlessly, still staring at her intensely. "Which naturally accounts for your great interest in the office and what I was doing there!"

"I know the truth now," she protested. "I know what you've been doing, you told me so yourself and I believed you. You've been doing it because Mr. Maynard refused to allow you any more to spend on the station. That was *not* my doing, Pat. Please believe me."

"The money from here –"

"I haven't had much from Gum Valley at all."

"You've had plenty, Miss Carrington-Smythe, I know that."

"Don't call me that," she cried piteously.

"It's your name, isn't it?" he asked furiously. "You're the woman who has ignored us all during the past years, who never bothered to come and find out for yourself what your inheritance was doing for you. By your own admission you didn't even know where Gum Valley was! You're the woman who caused me to twist figures and accounts to gain a little extra for what we needed, because of you I've put myself on the wrong side of the law. Then, when you did come, you arrived under an assumed name, tried to make yourself pleasant and starting delving into something you knew nothing about and consequently put the wrong construction upon it." He lowered his voice and looked at her in a manner which reminded her forcibly of the cold-eyed man who had met her at Murra Creek, the rude casual Pat Kennedy she had nearly forgotten. "How many times did I tell you I hated Miss Carrington-Smythe? How many times did you sit and listen as I abused her? Why didn't you say anything then? Why did you let it drift along for so long?"

"Because I discovered I loved you," said Anne softly.

His lips twisted bitterly. "You wouldn't have done this to me if you'd loved me."

"I didn't," she cried wildly. "Not when I first came here. But it's grown so gradually, so sweetly – Oh, Pat!"

"Butterflies have such shallow little hearts they can't be capable of any depth of feeling. You said you were tired of your friends, of the life you were leading. Maybe you would have soon tired of me and the life out here. Do you mean to tell me that these months at Gum Valley have wiped out entirely from your mind the habit of years, the years you spent travelling the world, indulging in every little whim? Do you mean to tell me you haven't wanted the polished manners and pretty speeches of the men who used to accompany you to all the affairs you must have attended? Because if you tell me that I shan't believe you!"

"I haven't missed anything," she answered desperately, stung by the scorn in his voice. "Believe it or not, but I've been happy here, perfectly happy. The only thing that worried me was what I should say when the time came for me to tell you the truth."

"Now I know." He looked her up and down and her hands fell to her sides and she lowered her head to hide her tear-filled eyes. It was no use arguing with him when he was in this difficult mood; the shock of discovery had wiped everything else from his mind. Perhaps later, when he had time to think things over, when he had slept upon the idea and become more used to it, then he might calm down a little and realise she had still been Anne Carrington-Smythe when she had confessed her love for him. Whoever she was or whatever he said that fact could not be gainsaid.

"The owner of Gum Valley," he went on, and as if the thought had become too much for him Pat raised his voice and flung words at her, words that revealed his hurt and the blow to his pride. So far he had been coldly polite and bitterly scornful; now he became hostile, and as she listened Anne cowered back against the table. "No wonder you couldn't cook," he stormed. "No wonder you were such an idiot with the sewing machine! It's my bet you'd never used one before in your life. You'd never worked, never given a thought to the men who worked for you. You don't deserve Gum Valley and all it holds. I've been a fool too, a big one, I should have had more sense than to stay here, working all the hours God sends for a woman like you. I've finished here," he concluded wrathfully. "You can get some other fool to take my place –"

"You can't leave now," she cried aghast. "You can't do this to me! What could I do at Gum Valley without you here?"

He shrugged his shoulders. "That no longer concerns me. You've made your bed, Miss Carrington-Smythe, now you can lie on it!"

"Pat!"

"Don't Pat me!" he exclaimed irritably. "I won't go on working for a woman who's so deceitful, who does such things as you've done behind my back. I'm going today."

"You can't. The river –"

"I shall get over the creek before it floods the road. If it's already come over I'll still get through!" And looking at him Anne could well believe what he said. He looked angry enough to tackle anything, as if he had only to storm against the river and it would fall back into its bed to give him right of way.

"And Mr. Norton?" she asked, her hand to her throat.

"He'll go with me, naturally. And if Mr. Maynard arrives, I can safely guess that he'll be coming soon –" he glanced at her face. "Yes, I thought so! So he *is* coming? I shall be at home if the police want to arrest me for embezzlement."

"And Joy?" she asked again.

He had forgotten his niece and his face changed its expression. The child could not be endangered on that muddy slippery road in the pouring rain, the chances were that he would have to struggle over the wooden bridge as it was. Mr. Norton could follow him, he was a man, physically capable of a few hard knocks, but the child was a different proposition altogether. Another wave of fury swept through him, now he had said he was going he wanted to get away from the place as quickly as possible.

A car door was heard to slam and he spun round.

"Now, who the blazes is this?" he asked violently, striding out of the room, leaving Anne, with tears running down her face, staring at the battered suitcase. Faintly she heard footsteps, heard Pat's voice, still shaking with fury, ask curtly,

"Who are you? If you're selling anything, we don't want it!"

"Ah!" cried another voice triumphantly. "You must be the insolent Mr. Kennedy!"

"Mother!" Anne dashed through the door, down the hall and out on to the verandah. "Oh, Mother!"

The next moment she was in her mother's arms, clinging to her desperately. In those few moments Mrs. Smythe had seen the misery on her daughter's face and she raised her eyes to study the man staring at her in stupefaction.

"You've been having another argument?" she asked, holding her daughter tightly. Pat nodded slowly and she smiled. "You've been having arguments all the time she has been here, haven't you?" Looking down, she patted Anne's shoulders. "Oh, pet, I could have told you that the course of true love never did run smooth!"

CHAPTER SEVEN

FOR THE rest of the day it rained steadily, the clouds were so low and it was so dark that it became necessary to switch on lights and occasionally the wind would rise suddenly and bend the tops of the trees in fantastic arcs. Radio broadcasts told of a rapid rise the whole way back along its winding course, the weather forecasts warned of more rain and of flooding upon all the inland streams and rivers, but it was the Macquarie which mattered most to the small community at Gum Valley. The tributaries had already broken their banks, roads were cut one by one, and properties, large and small, were being isolated by the hour.

Personally Pat was thankful he had so much to do, and as the afternoon wore on he was relieved to think Joy's presence had halted his first wild angry impulse to leave. He was a natural leader and the men followed his orders without question, knowing that perhaps their very lives depended upon what they did at his bidding. If he had struggled through to Murra Creek he would have been tormented by the thought that he had deserted his post at a critical time and would have spent his time wondering frantically what was happening in their isolation and if everyone was safe and well. Wet to the skin, with water trickling down his neck from the brim of his ancient hat, he worked with the others on the last of the fences, letting down the netting to allow the flood waters with the accompanying debris to have free access over the land.

Raising his head, Pat stood up and leaned wearily against the shovel he had been using, straining his eyes as he tried to peer through the mist caused by the heavy rain. There was little to see, the nearest trees were nearly obliterated by the misty atmosphere, the tall brown grass was beaten flat and there was mud and water everywhere. As another gust of wind swept across the paddock he bent to work again.

"Damn everything!" he cried ferociously, and young Dick, working nearby, looked at him anxiously.

Weary in every limb, the five of them finally made their way to the waiting cart, drawn by two wet patient horses and flung their shovels and tools into the back.

Keen eyes surveyed the state of the land as the cart moved at a slow pace along the track, and where it swung towards the river a new sound became evident above the wind and the rain. They looked quickly at each other, Peter reined in and with one accord they turned towards the bank.

"Look at it," whispered Dick.

The sound was of water rushing through the trunks of the gum trees, for during the hours they had been toiling in the paddocks the river had risen rapidly and was now swirling through the trees and foliage with the soft swish reminiscent of the surf on the coastal beaches. Pat glanced at the sky; it was still thick and heavy with cloud, there was not a break to be seen anywhere and from it rain fell steadily and monotonously. Jan caught his glance and the two of them looked again at the river.

"How long does it take the water to come down from Bathurst, Wellington and Dubbo?" he asked quietly.

"A week, maybe more."

They were silent, realising that the river had by no means reached its peak, that the flow would go on increasing in volume until it became a raging torrent in the centre of the stream and it would stay like that, cutting them off from the world, for as long as it rained along the river's length.

Pat was too preoccupied at the moment to even think of Anne, his personal troubles were fading into the background as he realised how serious this was going to be for Gum Valley and all the people living there. A week before the river began to subside, maybe more; another week before the roads were fit to travel on, and even then there would be wide detours through other people's property as the hollows in the track would still be under water, that made a fortnight. Two weeks of anxiety.

What was worrying him chiefly was the bluff near the homestead. Once that went there would be nothing to stop the swift flow of water from entering the back entrance of Gum Valley. Unless a retainer wall was made round the whole garden. Mentally he groaned at the thought of the work involved; even Alan and Mr. Norton would have to assist, for time was getting short. He looked down at the dirty weary faces of his companions. and sighed. They had done enough for today, he could not ask them for anything else. There was a limit to what men could stand, and after eight hours' solid work, standing ankle deep, sometimes more, in water, with the wind and rain beating on their bodies – he shook his head. Tomorrow might not be too late.

The cart came to an abrupt stop a few yards from the bank and Pat leapt to the ground, going on alone towards the edge. During a previous flood part of this bank had collapsed and now it rose sheer from the water's edge to a height of about twenty-five feet. He caught his breath when he saw the water was only two or three feet from the top. Another night and this part of Gum Valley would be inundated. The land dropped slightly from the bank away from the direction of the house and the bulk of the water would rush across the paddocks towards the railway line, many miles away.

Pat sighed. After this the river bank would take on a different appearance altogether. The bed of the stream would be choked with fallen trees and new channels would be made, where it had been shallow it would run deep, and the holes in the river bed would be filled with shifting sand. The many beaches would disappear and reappear again in another place altogether, those that had been of sand would probably be a mass of pebbles and the willows which graced the low banks would in many places vanish completely from sight.

"Come on," shouted Rusty impatiently. "You look as though you're staying there all night!"

"There's nothing I could do even if I did stay all night," said Pat as he rejoined them. "It will be over before morning."

"And probably wash the track away like it did last time," grumbled the groom. "Remember the first time we went into town after the last flood, Jan? We had to make our own road and were getting on nicely until we hit a soft spot and the ground collapsed under our wheels!"

Jan nodded, watching Dick's face. "What's the matter?"

Dick started and his face flushed under the grime. "You'll think me crazy," he muttered, "but I'm sure I heard voices –"

"*Voices?*" they interrupted him with one accord, and he nodded.

"Yes. From down the track. Listen a moment, when the wind drops a little, I'm sure I'm right."

He was very much in earnest and after gazing at him for a moment Pat held up his hand in silence and the five of them strained their ears in the direction he had indicated. There was the moan of the wind through the trees, the rush of water through the trunks of the gums, the heavy rain and the impatient pawing of the ground by one of the horses. Nothing else.

"You must have been mistaken," said Pat relaxing.

"No!" Dick was emphatic. "The wind is coming this way – listen."

This time they all heard a man's voice coming through the mist and they gaped at each other in bewilderment.

"What on earth –" began Pat, but did not finish his sentence. Peter gave a jerk on the reins and the horses, greatly relieved that they were to move at last, started off quickly and the jackaroo nearly lost his balance. He gave Peter a baleful glance and the other looked at him a trifle grimly.

"I heard a woman's voice," he said. "Anne can't be out here –"

"I'll wring her neck if she is!" threatened Pat, his heart giving an uneven leap. Surely Anne had more sense than to wander so far from the homestead when it was beginning to grow dark.

Four people came into sight, staggering over the wet uneven ground. Two men were holding up another and beside them walked a girl, as he looked at her the gleam of amusement flickered in Pat's eyes. For she was wearing very high-heeled shoes and she rocked upon them, her stockings were black with mud splashes and the light grey coat she was wearing was wet through and clung tightly to her figure. At the sight of the cart with its rough-looking occupants she gave a little scream and was curtly told to shut up by the younger man. He waved thankfully and the man he was helping lifted his head and gave a sigh of relief.

Pat jumped down, followed by Rusty and Jan and went towards the little group.

"Thank heaven we've met someone," cried the young man. "We're just about all in –"

"Our car bogged," sobbed the girl, tottering on her feet. "And we've walked for miles. This rain and the *road* –" her voice faded away and despite her discomfort she frowned at the look on the face of the tall man facing her. With two days' growth on his chin, with mud and water on his cheeks and with his hair hanging over his forehead, Pat looked a ruffian, but so did the others for that matter. Only Dick, who rarely shaved, was reasonably presentable, and his face looked youthful and trusting.

"Is this Gum Valley?" asked the man in the centre of the three, his companions were still holding him and one foot dragged behind a little, as he tried to straighten up a spasm of pain increased his features.

The jackaroo nodded. "This is Gum Valley. But surely you haven't come out here on purpose to look round the place in weather such as this?"

"I don't really know *why* we've come," moaned the girl. "I would never have consented to make the trip if I'd known –"

"Oh, be quiet!" snapped the third man, who, up to now, had not spoken. "You've done nothing but moan and squeal ever since the car bogged. About three miles further back," he added for the benefit of the others.

"Anne?" asked the youngest man eagerly. "Is she here?"

Pat looked hard into the other's face, his own inscrutable. "Miss Carrington-Smythe?" he asked coolly, and felt rather than saw the starts of surprise from Rusty and Jan. "Yes, she's here."

The man in the centre of the group was looking at them with keen eyes and his gaze returned to the tall figure standing before him. It was obvious he was the leader of the others.

"My name is Maynard," he said quietly, and Pat lifted his head.

"I thought you would be coming – some time. But I didn't expect you quite so soon. I'm Kennedy."

*

128

Mrs. Carrington-Smythe had been a sympathetic listener as her daughter, kneeling on the floor beside her chair, had sobbed out the whole story. From time to time she nodded in agreement, once or twice a smile had come and gone quickly across her face, and finally she lifted Anne's face gently between her hands and kissed her.

"I'm glad I came, pet," she said softly. "For between you, you seem to have made an awful mess of things!"

"And it's all my doing," whispered Anne. "I should have been more interested in what Uncle left me and I shouldn't have deceived Pat as I did. When I first came and he was so rude to me – well, what would anyone have thought under the circumstances? Wasn't it natural I should blame him? On the surface everything looked as if he was the culprit. Now the money doesn't matter, I wish I hadn't any. He has every right to be annoyed with me, but oh, Mother, if you could have heard him this morning! He was wild, I've never seen him in such a temper and he called me every name he could think of!"

"He'll be sorry about that later, when he's had time to think it over," said her mother comfortingly.

"He threatened to leave here –" Anne gulped.

"That was all said in the heat of the moment. Now he can't leave he'll probably change his mind –"

"Oh!" Anne leapt suddenly to her feet. "The men's dinners! And Joy – I wonder where she is." She hugged her mother quickly and ran towards the door. "Come over to the kitchen if you want me. I must go – that child –"

"Which child? Whose child?" Mrs. Smythe watched her daughter's hurried exit. "Whatever is a child doing at Gum Valley?"

Left to her own devices she fetched a case from the back of her car, and after depositing it in the hall wandered through the many rooms which brought back nostalgic memories of the holidays she had spent here with her husband. She looked thoughtfully at the single bed which was placed beside the double one in Anne's room, wondering again about the child, who was she, what was she doing here, who did she belong to?

"Are you Anne's mother?" enquired a little voice at the door, and spinning round she said,

"Why, yes. But who are you?"

"Joy. Uncle Pat is my uncle." The child smiled. "Anne told me to tell you that dinner is ready. The men have had theirs, they were in such a rush because they had to go back to the fences. Isn't the flood exciting? I suppose I shall have to wash myself," she added as though the thought of water had reminded her she was very grubby.

"I think that's necessary," remarked the other with a laugh. "How have you got so dirty?"

"I've been helping Alan in the garden. Do you want a wash too?"

Together they went through to the bathroom and later, sheltered under a huge umbrella, made their way across to the kitchen. Mrs. Smythe looked round with great interest, trying to imagine the elegant Anne working and working happily in these surroundings. The girl was standing by the draining board, making a neat pile of the dirty plates, and she was biting her lips as though to keep back her tears. Throughout the meal, Pat had ignored her, he had not spoken a word to any of the men and had been the first to leave the room.

Another hot meal was prepared for the evening, for she could well imagine how tired and hungry the men would be when they returned. The rain continued to beat monotonously on the iron roof, drowning the radio which had been left on so that she could hear the latest reports from the various points along the river's length. It told a sorry story. The Macquarie was flooding rich pasture land on either bank for many miles, people were being rescued from their homes by boats, and damage to houses and property was being reported every hour. Once Anne noticed Joy peering out of the window with a look of fear on her face and felt a feeling of panic in her own heart. There were no hills around Gum Valley, no higher ground they could rush to if necessary, and she wished they had not the child with them.

"Uncle's late," she murmured fretfully. "It's nearly dark."

"They're all on their way home now," said Anne soothingly, putting her arm round the girl's shoulders and peering with her out of the window. "Listen —"

"The horses! Don't they sound tired? And won't Rusty be cross because he has to put them to bed before he can have his tea!" Joy giggled heartlessly and forgot her fear of a moment before.

The horses and cart came into view in the dull light and Anne frowned.

"There seem to be a great many people sitting there!" she exclaimed. "I wonder if someone got bogged on the road? Four, five — why, there are seven or eight. One looks like a girl, I can't see properly."

Joy had rushed to open the door and Anne gave her mother a suspicious glance; Mrs. Smythe shook her head quickly, denying all knowledge of the newcomers. Above the rain they could hear Rusty's voice, swearing loudly. Peter was standing up with the reins in his hands and Pat and Jan were helping a stranger to the ground. Another stranger jumped lightly down and held out his hands to the slight figure beneath the numerous wheat sacks, Anne gave an audible gasp as the girl whimpered, then someone else was by her side, his arms went round her and she received a resounding kiss.

"Hello, sweet! If this doesn't surprise you nothing ever will!"

"*Roddie!*" Her face went white and she clutched the door behind her for support.

"In person." His devil-may-care eyes were laughing at her

wickedly as he kissed her again, totally unconscious of the others staring at him. Anne allowed herself to be hugged, too surprised and shocked by his sudden appearance to push him away, and over his shoulder she saw Pat watching her. He gave her a look which chilled her to the bone as he made sure Mr. Maynard could hobble into the kitchen and then turned away.

"I'll attend to the horses," he said curtly to Rusty. "You can go and get changed."

"Thank heaven for that!" snapped the groom, who was in a thorough bad temper. But before he left he put his hand on Pat's arm. "Who is Miss Carrington-Smythe?"

"The cook," was the abrupt reply.

There were low whistles of astonishment from the men, cut short by the girl's shrill voice as she was assisted into the kitchen.

"How on earth you can live in such a *terrible* place is beyond me!"

"Barbara!" Anne gasped, and glanced wildly from one face to another. "Mr. Maynard and Mr. Jeen. Oh, why have you come?" and to the consternation of everyone but Mrs. Smythe she shook herself free from Roddie and burst into tears as she fled from the room.

"This is certainly going to complicate matters!" said Mrs. Smythe to herself, and then moved forward into the crowd of people in the doorway. "Good evening, Mr. Maynard, I certainly didn't expect to see you here."

"And I didn't expect to see you, dear Mrs. Smythe," he shook hands warmly. "This is my partner, Mr. Jeen, and I think you already know – er – Miss Hainsworth." By the tone of his voice Mr. Maynard sounded to be annoyed with Miss Hainsworth.

"I know both Roddie *and* Barbara," she said pointedly, and a little smile flitted over the solicitor's tired face. "But tell me, why have you come?"

"The call of duty, Mrs. Smythe. I've been – er – worried

about your daughter and the goings on, shall I say, at Gum Valley. It was my intention to straighten things out for Miss Carrington-Smythe, but we didn't, unfortunately, anticipate this deluge when we left Sydney."

Mrs. Smythe glanced at them each in turn. They were all wet through and looked tired, the solicitor especially. She had always liked Mr. Maynard, a more honest and trustworthy man she had yet to meet, but she did not think so highly of his partner. Mr. Jeen was a big well-made man, more suited, she would have thought, to the boxing ring than to a solicitor's office.

"I think," she said slowly, "that the best plan would be for you all to come with me to the homestead and have baths. The men can then get their meal and I daresay Anne will be able to find something for you. You must all be very hungry."

Roddie looked at her curiously. "Is Anne supposed to be the cook here? Mr. Maynard explained something about it, but I really thought he was pulling my leg!"

"Anne *is* the cook, she's not supposed to be at all!"

He grinned, "This must be seen to be believed."

"Oh, Roddie," wailed Barbara, "don't start asking questions now. I'm soaked, and my poor *feet*! I shall never be able to walk again. Let's do as Mrs. Smythe suggests and get out of this awful room, I'm sure there must be a better place elsewhere. And our cases," her voice rose sharply. "They're in the car. How are we going to manage without those? Someone must go back for them, I *must* have clean dry clothes."

"We must all have dry clothes," agreed Mr. Jeen. He looked round the kitchen, felt the warmth of the fire and his nose twitched at the appetising smell coming from the oven. "And we must have a meal. Where is Miss Carrington-Smythe? She's the owner here and will give the necessary orders about our cases. One of those men will have to return."

Mrs. Smythe snorted gently. "Those men have been out in

the rain all day, they're tired and are ready for something to eat –"

"So are we!" exclaimed Barbara sharply. She was quite unnerved by the experience of being bogged so near the flooding river and of having to walk at least three miles through mud and slime in her flimsy shoes. "Our clothes! I *must* have my case."

"I don't know who you are and I don't particularly care," remarked an unfeeling voice behind her. "But I do wish you would stop whining about your case. Suitcases," continued Pat, thrusting his hands into his pockets and leaning back against the door, "have caused a great deal of trouble in this part of the world."

They all turned and Mrs. Smythe had her first good look at the jackaroo. In her mind's eye she wiped his face clean of the mud and water, removed the blueness from around his chin and upper lip, dressed him in clean clothes and was mentally pleased at the result. He looked a real man, he would be at once masterful and tender, just the type Anne needed to keep her in hand. He would stand no nonsense from her, he would argue and lose his temper with her and at the same time he would love her deeply and unwaveringly. Any doubts Mrs. Smythe had entertained about the wisdom of her daughter's choice fled from her and she smiled at him approvingly. Pat saw the smile and against his will he smiled back. Here he had met an unexpected ally if ever he needed one.

"I don't think there's any need for such remarks, Kennedy," cried Mr. Jeen, looking at him down his nose. "Someone must return for those suitcases tonight."

Pat looked them all over and nodded his head. Someone would have to go out to the bogged car on that terrible track, and if they did not go tonight it would be too late.

"I'll see you get your cases," he promised grimly.

"Who will you send?" asked Mr. Maynard curiously.

"I'll go myself."

"You will not," said Anne, coming back into the room. Her face was white and she had regained a little of her composure after the shock of seeing Roddie and the others, but her heart felt like a solid piece of ice in her breast. Pat had seen Roddie's welcome, and that on top of Mr. Maynard's unexpected and untimely arrival would make her task of explaining well nigh impossible. "No one is going back all that way for your cases tonight."

Mr. Jeen, Mr. Maynard and Barbara tried to tell her at once how essential it was they had their belongings. Roddie sat on the nearest chair and placed his arms along the back, watching the changing expressions on the various faces with amusement.

Pat finally made himself heard. "Miss Carrington-Smythe, I *am* going back. The river is near the top of the bank and before morning the bogged car will be under water."

"Very well," said Anne, in a voice as cold as his. "If you insist on going I shall go with you."

"Don't be a fool!" he cried angrily in reply, and Mr. Maynard cried "Tut-tut!" beneath his breath.

"Seeing that it's my car," said Roddie mildly, "I think I'm entitled to return with Kennedy."

"A wonderful idea," agreed Mrs. Smythe enthusiastically as she imagined these two together for an hour or so. "That's settled, then! Barbara, do you think you can stagger a few yards further? We'll go to the house and let the men have their meal – this way, Mr. Maynard."

She shepherded them into the darkness hastily and they were only too eager to go with her. Roddie sauntered after them, leaving Anne and Pat in the kitchen. Pat caught sight of Joy sitting quietly in a corner and frowned.

"Why aren't you in bed?" he asked abruptly.

"I've been waiting for you," she faltered. Uncle Pat looked

different tonight. She could not quite explain his expression, but she did not like it, and tears welled up in her eyes. Anne saw them and ran across the room.

"Uncle Pat is tired," she explained quietly. "Run after the others and I'll come and tuck you up as soon as I've given the men their tea." Joy hurried out and Anne straightened herself. "Pat, even if you are annoyed with me there's no need to take it out of the child."

"I'm not annoyed," he began, and stopped. Annoyance was not what he felt. Mentally he was embittered and disillusioned, physically he was exhausted, the combination made him feel light-headed and he did not want to talk to Anne or anyone else. Because her love for him was so deep and understanding she knew how he felt and so did not argue with him; her voice when she spoke was low and unhurried.

"You'd better wait and have your meal before you go out again." She turned as the men came in one by one, decidedly cleaner and still weary-looking. "How are you going down to the car?"

"I'll use the tractor. If it will go," he added with great feeling as he sat down with the rest. When she had placed the plates on the table Anne withdrew to one corner and began to plan another meal. She frowned as she banked up the fire and tested the heat of the oven with her hand before placing a large dish containing numerous chops in the warm interior, wondering why Roddie had seen fit to drive out to Gum Valley. If he had come for an answer to the question he had asked before she left Sydney she was afraid he was going to be very disappointed. Devoutedly she wished he had stayed in the city; his arrival could not have been more inopportune. Neither was she pleased to see Mr. Maynard and she was determined to give him a piece of her mind for disobeying her instructions at the first opportunity.

Pat, still in his damp clothes, was the first to leave the room, and within a few minutes they heard the staccato note from the tractor's engine.

"Where's he going now?" asked Dick curiously.

"To fetch the cases from the car."

"He can go for all I care," muttered Rusty. "Not for Pat or anyone else am I going out again tonight. We've done more than enough today, when I suggested we came home earlier in the afternoon he snapped my head off. As if I care what happens to Gum Valley!" He recollected suddenly that he was in the presence of his employer. "I *beg* your pardon, Miss Carrington-Smythe," he said sarcastically, and flounced out of the room. Anne looked at the others.

"Rusty is tired and bad-tempered." A smile crossed her own tired face. "Please, don't let this make any difference to you. I'm still Miss Smith and shall continue here as cook until we can make other arrangements. After that," she lifted her head, "I'm going to live in the homestead."

The evening passed quickly and there was no time for brooding over what had happened during the momentous day. After the hot meal had been carried well covered from the rain, to the house, Anne left them to it, said goodnight to Joy and started to rearrange the sleeping accommodation. Barbara would have to share a room with her mother because she did not intend Pat being turned out of his own room. The two solicitors shared another and Roddie would have to sleep on one of the verandahs.

Barbara was still inclined to be peevish after dinner and spoke to Anne only when it was necessary. She did not argue when shown her room, but gave a deep significant sigh at the sight of the two beds.

Mr. Maynard was nursing his twisted ankle and had started to sneeze.

"He always gets a cold when he gets wet," stated Mr. Jeen. "Tomorrow he'll most probably have a sore throat."

"I hope not." Anne looked down at her solicitor. "Mr. Maynard, why did you come when I specifically asked you not to? Didn't you get the letter I wrote just after Christmas?"

"Yes, Miss Carring –"

"Miss Smith."

"All right, if you prefer it that way. I did receive your letter," he went on in his precise voice. "And it was because of that I – er – decided to make this trip and find out for myself what was happening. You and your family have always been good clients, I only wanted to do what I thought best in your interests and to my mind your ignorance of station matters was being played upon by that man Kennedy. It would be quite easy to deceive you, dear Miss – er – Smith, and, after Mr. Jeen had seen through the books again, we're convinced that that's exactly what he has been doing. The accounts must have been altered –"

"I know," said Anne wearily, sitting down beside her mother. "He juggles with them, adds a little bit here and takes away a little bit there –"

"What *are* you talking about?" asked Mr. Jeen angrily.

"I'm telling you that I know what's been going on. And I have only myself to blame. Or rather," she looked at them quizzically, "I blame myself for not taking more notice of what you two have been doing."

"Miss Carrington-Smythe!" Mr. Maynard sat bolt upright in his chair. "Are you insinuating –"

"That you've been tampering with the accounts too? No. But the fault has been ours, shall I put it that way? Pat – Mr. Kennedy – would have had no cause to alter any accounts if more money had been made available for working expenses. I knew nothing of that and I wasn't told. All he has taken has been used for the benefit of the place and not for his own personal gains."

"You have no proof of that," cried Mr. Jeen.

"Only his word."

He laughed insinuatingly and the colour stained her cheeks again.

"Easy, pet," murmured Mrs. Smythe warningly, and her daughter relaxed.

"You're right, Mother. I think we'd better leave any discussions about Gum Valley's finances until later. Mr. Maynard looks very tired and there'll be plenty of time during the next ten days or so to get this straightened out."

"Ten days, did you say?" asked Mr. Jeen weakly.

"Easily that. The river hasn't yet reached its peak and when it does the road will be cut in more places than one. The men tell me that after the last flood they couldn't get into town for nearly three weeks."

Both men stared at her in horror, then Mr. Maynard took a grip on himself.

"I sincerely hope Miss Hainsworth will bear that blow with tranquillity," he cried.

"Tell me, please, why Mr. Hall and Miss Hainsworth came with you? I asked you not to tell anyone where I was or what I was doing."

"My apologies, Miss Smith. But Mr. Hall came to me and explained that you were – er – be married –"

"Oh!" Scarlet-faced, Anne stared at him.

"And," he went on placidly, "he pleaded to be told where you were staying because he wished to see you regarding the wedding, which I understand is to take place after your return to Sydney. Miss Hainsworth had evidently coaxed the truth out of him and decided to come with us."

"I am *not* returning to Sydney and there will be no wedding!" said Anne angrily. Roddie had taken too much for granted and this would have to be pointed out to him as quickly as possible. She wondered miserably what he was saying to Pat at this very moment. The two of them were alone miles from the homestead and it would be natural for conversation to be limited, at the beginning, to Gum Valley, and from there it would turn towards herself. Deperately she hoped Pat was still in a difficult mood. Answering questions with those curt monosyllables would be quite sufficient to dry up any conversation.

She waited alone for the return of the tractor and it was turned eleven o'clock before she heard it in the distance. Going out on to the verandah she watched the headlights draw nearer, thinking they were remarkably clear, and it was then she realised it had stopped raining.

The tractor stopped by the gate, the car pulled up behind and two figures bent over the front mudguard. Then she heard a curt "Goodnight," the tractor rumbled away and Roddie came alone up the path.

"Has it been very difficult?" asked Anne quietly as he stepped on to the verandah.

"It has," he paused by her side, his shoulders drooping. "We had to dig out the car, then the tractor got bogged and I believe it was only because the jackaroo lost his temper with it that it went at all! It must have been so startled at the words he flung at it that it jumped clean back on to the track again! Until then I don't think he had spoken half a dozen words – what a taciturn man he is!" he added, and put his head on her shoulder. "Anne, I'm so tired."

"In which case you'd better go to bed," she answered briskly. "I've put you on the verandah, Roddie, but the bed is comfortable and you'll be quite dry. Also there's something to eat."

"You know, you don't sound very enthusiastic over my arrival," he complained. "I've come a long way to see you."

"I didn't expect you."

"All the more reason why you should have been delightfully surprised." He looked into her face. "You're changed, Anne, you aren't quite the girl I knew before."

"Perhaps not," she agreed slowly. He had turned towards the

door and was waiting expectantly, but she lingered, looking out towards the sheds. "Isn't Pat coming?"

"Kennedy went to put the tractor away. Evidently it has to be carefully nursed, if it isn't it ceases to function. He remarked there was more rain coming. Come along and show me the food I'm more than ready for it."

Roddie was having a shower when Pat came quietly into the house. He went to his old room intending to collect his clothes before moving back to the men's quarters and was fully prepared when he turned on the light to see the room either occupied by one of the solicitors or with Mr. Hall's possessions scattered about. But the room was exactly as he had left it early that morning, nothing had been disturbed and it was empty.

"Supper is ready in the sitting room," said Anne quietly behind him, and as he turned to face her she cried out with concern, "Oh, Pat, you do look tired!"

"I'm all right." He indicated the room with a wave of his hand. "I thought you would be needing this for one of your guests."

"That's your room."

"I'm going back to the quarters."

"There's no need –"

"I'm going back to the quarters," he repeated stubbornly.

"Not tonight," she said firmly.

Pat compressed his lips and folded his arms. "Starting to give orders already, are you, Miss Carrington –"

"If you call me that again," she cried in a trembling voice, "I'll – I'll hit you!"

"As you please." By the tone of his voice she gathered that she was quite at liberty to hit him if she wished, he could not care less. "But I'm still going."

"You are not!" Anne stamped her foot. "You're too tired to trail across there. Everything is ready for you here, I have supper prepared –"

"I don't want any," and added ungraciously, "Thanks."

She looked at him and the storminess died out of her eyes. He looked so cross and tired, like a boy with his rumpled hair and dirty cheeks, and the impulse to shake him, then kiss him soundly, was almost irresistible.

From the sitting room came the sound of a teaspoon rattling in a saucer, Roddie began to whistle softly and Pat drew himself up.

"Mr. Hall is waiting for you," he said indifferently. "Don't let me keep you."

Anne seemed to sag against the wall. No wonder he did not want any supper; he was not going to sit in their own room with Roddie present. It was useless arguing further with him, he was too remote, as far away from her as though he was on the far bank of the ever-widening river.

"Promise me you'll sleep here," she whispered.

Pat gave in; he was too weary to do anything else. He nodded and went through the open doorway. "Goodnight."

Slowly Anne retraced her steps to the sitting room where Roddie had made himself quite at home, he had poured out the tea and was already deep into the pile of sandwiches she had prepared.

"So you like Gum Valley," he said by way of an opening when it became obvious she did not intend starting a conversation.

"So much that I'm never going to leave it," was the quiet answer.

His hand halted half way to his mouth. "Never?"

"Never."

"I see." Roddie nibbled round the edges of another sandwich. "Was that very emphatic word intended to warn me that I must not ask you to return to Sydney with me? Keep off the grass, so to speak."

Anne nodded. "Yes. I'm sorry, Roddie."

He drained his cup, peeped into hers, and when he saw it half full poured out another drink for himself. "By that I gather your feelings towards me haven't changed? Absence hasn't worked its usual miracle?"

"No." She hated to do this because she was genuinely fond of Roddie, but he must be made to understand that as far as he was concerned there would be no wedding. Passing her hand through her hair she leaned back against the cushions. It had been a terrific day, full of emotional strain, hard work and unexpected surprises, and the combination had tired her completely. Roddie crossed to her side and sat down, slipping an arm round her shoulders, as he did so tears started to her eyes and he shook her gently.

"You shouldn't be crying, Anne. As a rejected suitor that's my privilege." He looked at her closely. "Is the coming flood upsetting you?"

"No." But in fairness to Roddie, who loved her, she could not go into explanations about the cause of her unhappiness. "I mean, yes."

"Make up your mind! You're tired too," he said suddenly, courteously offering her a handkerchief as she sniffed. "What time do you get up in the morning?"

"Just before six."

"Good lord! In which case you'd better trot off to bed without delay." He helped her to her feet and smiled down into her eyes. "Don't be broken-hearted about me, old thing, I'm not the type to brood, nor am I likely to throw myself into the raging river –"

"You're a dear, Roddie," she said brokenly. "Some day, someone is going to have a very nice husband."

"Would I sound conceited if I said I agreed with you?" he kissed her lightly. "I just wish – oh, never mind, you trot off."

He watched her go and absently picked up the last sandwich.

This he carried with him on to the verandah and standing near his bed he looked out across the garden.

The sandwich finished, he withdrew a gold cigarette case from his jacket pocket and absently lighted a cigarette. Thoughtfully he blew a smoke ring into the damp air, refusing to believe Gum Valley was the only reason for Anne's decision to stay, and remembered Pat Kennedy. His forehead creased in a frown. Surely Anne had not fallen in love with that tall dark man with the cold grey eyes. If she had, he himself had been guilty of a great indiscretion, for hadn't he jumped off that confounded cart and hugged and kissed her in front of everyone as though he had a perfect right? Roddie straightened himself. If he had put a spanner in the works as regards Anne and the jackaro, he would have to do his best to rectify matters, for he wanted her to be happy.

CHAPTER EIGHT

Mr. Norton yawned, looked out of the window and yawned again. It was still raining, not quite as heavily as it had been doing the previous day, and the clouds did not look as heavy. He dressed slowly and carefully, taking a long time over his shaving and the arrangement of his tie, and after placing his violin in its case with loving care, he opened the door and stepped outside.

Keeping under the shelter of the verandah and then of the pepper trees, he made his way to the kitchen, but paused before opening the door. Mild surprise flickered in his eyes as he gazed towards the homestead, for there seemed to be a great number of people working in the garden, digging energetically, moving rapidly and talking spasmodically. Mr. Norton looked puzzled.

As he watched and waited, wondering if he should find Pat and ask if it was in order for those strangers to walk over Alan's garden, the jackaroo himself came from the group towards the kitchen. Blood dripped from his left hand and Mr. Norton clicked his tongue.

"Now what have you been doing?"

"The spade slipped – it's nothing much, John," he added quickly, noticing the look on the manager's face. Blood always reminded Mr. Norton of a long hospital ward where he had spent a number of weeks, much against his will, for he had explained carefully to the doctors and nurses that he preferred being at Gum Valley to being with them even if they were kind and gentle when his head ached.

"I'm going to wash it and stick a bandage round," continued Pat nonchalantly, wrapping a grubby handkerchief round the wound quickly and thrusting his hands behind his back.

Mr. Norton looked back to the garden. "I was going to ask if it's necessary for all those people to walk over Alan's garden. He'll be annoyed, you know."

"We're digging a retainer wall," explained the other with his customary patience when talking to the manager. "The river has risen very rapidly during the night and the water is beginning to creep over the bank in one or two places opposite the back of the house."

"So it is!" Mr. Norton looked startled as he noticed it for the first time. "Dear me! Who are all those people anyway? I don't remember having seen them before." He frowned with a great effort of concentration.

"No, they only arrived last night."

"Why have they come?"

They've come because Anne wrote and told a string of lies to her solicitor, thought Pat bitterly, and the young one came with them because he loved her and had known her in her other life. Why am I still slaving like this to save the place, when in another couple of weeks' time I shall be gone? he wondered wildly.

He did not answer Mr. Norton's question but asked one himself.

"John, do you know that for months now we've had with us

the owner of Gum Valley?" The manager looked interested.
"Yes, Miss Smith, the cook." His voice was bitter. "She's really
Miss Carrington-Smythe."

"I know."

"You know?" Pat stared at him in astonishment. "You
know? But how —"

"I recognised her," explained Mr. Norton. "Once, long ago,
I can't tell you when," he looked at Pat anxiously, "I met her.
I seem to remember a big room full of books, it was an office,
I think, and the old Boss was there with her. Undoubtedly it
was the same girl."

Pat knew of the sudden flashes of memory which sometime
tormented Mr. Norton by their very vagueness.

"Why didn't you tell me?" he asked rather savagely. "Why
didn't you ever say anything to me?"

"You never asked," said Mr. Norton rather plaintively.
"Should I have done?"

"I don't suppose it would have made any difference," said
Pat dully, and drew in his breath. Of course it would not have
made any difference; he would still have fallen in love with
Anne. She was the only person for him, the one woman he had
been waiting to find, cook or society girl, she was *his*. Then the
sudden light died out of his eyes, leaving them bleak and cold
again. That knowledge did not alter the fact that Roddie was
here, the suave good-looking young man who considered he had
a perfect right to put his arms round the girl and kiss her.

Mr. Norton spoke again. "But who are the men, Pat? And
that strange-looking woman over there? The one in the rubbers
and mackintosh."

"Anne's mother. Mrs. Smythe. You might have met her, too.
The big man is Mr. Jeen, a solicitor from Sydney. And the other
is a Mr. Hall. A friend of Miss Smith's."

Mr. Norton lost interest and continued on his way to a belated
breakfast.

In the afternoon Mrs. Smythe, who had been working with the rest filling wheat bags with soil on the retainer wall, stopped for a moment and leaned upon her shovel. Pat caught her glance and moved to her side.

"You've done sufficient," he said gruffly. "Why don't you leave it now, Mrs. Smythe?"

"I'm not working in the correct sense of the word," she confided, "being here chiefly to lend tone to the proceedings. You see, as long as I appear to be shovelling mud and filling bags neither Mr. Jeen nor Roddie have a good excuse to go and seek the comfort of the house. Both of them would do so as quickly as possible, for they aren't used to this kind of work."

They looked across to where Roddie was wearily lifting his shovel and Mr. Jeen was pulling at large blisters on his grubby hands. Pat grinned behind his hand.

"I hope," said Mrs. Smythe softly, looking round at the paddock nearby which was beginning to resemble a lake, "that no one has a grumbling appendix."

"So do I!" said her companion, fervently, thinking of the thirty-two-mile track into town. A good third would now be under water and even horses could not get through, as in parts it would be five or six feet deep.

"What would we do in a case like that?" she asked interestedly.

"Fix wings to the jeeps and have your daughter fly the patient out," came the prompt reply, and she laughed.

"That rankled, didn't it, Pat?"

"I'm afraid it did," he agreed slowly, looking at her. There was humour round the soft lips and in the brown eyes, yet the look she gave him was maternally understanding. He gained the impression that she liked him and was not adverse to her daughter linking her life with his.

Mrs. Smythe was watching his face and in the changing expressions she read a great deal.

"Learning to fly was only another way of trying to find the cause of her boredom," she said quietly.

"She might grow bored with anything in time," he suggested.

"I don't think so." She leaned more comfortably against the shovel. "Pat, after my husband died I was very lonely and wanted to wander, I simply couldn't settle in one place for any length of time. Anne was at school in Sydney and when she left she joined me in Queensland, after which she decided she would have a home of her own. She had money, and as she was capable of looking after herself I was quite agreeable to the idea. The home alone was not sufficient and she began to drift with the crowd, but she wasn't happy, for she had no definite object in view. I've got the knack of reading between the lines of her letters." Here she darted a mischievous glance in his direction. "And I know why she suddenly decided to get a job. You know the rest —"

"It doesn't excuse the fact that she'd forgotten Gum Valley," he cried, staring out across the water.

"That was unforgivable," she agreed. "Now she has found it, though, she won't leave it. This is the niche she has been looking for in life and I can understand her love for the place. It's in her blood — my people were farmers in Warwickshire, had been for generations, her father's people had always been on the land, and Claude Carrington-Smythe carried on all the old traditions by coming to a new country and working this little place up from nothing to what it is now." She waved her hand away from the river to the soaked paddocks.

"Why are you telling me all this?" asked Pat suddenly, and she had the grace to blush.

"Can't you guess?" she asked softly, and he laughed. Anne, coming from the house with a bully of tea and a trayful of cups, saw them together and her heart gave a sudden leap.

For the first time within days the sun showed a red streak of colour on the horizon when it set that evening, and the regular inhabitants of Gum Valley looked at it with relief. Usually a red sunset meant a warm day following, and this was the brightest sign they had seen in the sky for what seemed a very long time. But they knew, too, that more rain would fall, for clearing showers had been forecast on the radio and those at times could be violent, as much as half an inch of rain falling within half an hour.

It was a peculiar feeling, being cut off entirely from civilisation. Even the telephone was dead.

There was no boat at Gum Valley, and the one the old Boss had used years before had been drawn up on the bank and its timbers had rotted in the sun. There was nothing to enable any of them to get away and if the river continued its present rise things could become very unpleasant and uncomfortable. There was just one consolation, Pat thought, as he packed his pipe with tobacco and fumbled in his pockets for a box of matches, the higher the river rose the more it spread out in every direction, consequently it would not be very deep in the paddocks. Tomorrow he would have to take one of the horses and ride round, looking at the sheep and cattle. Most of them had been herded together and if the worst came to the worst they would have to be handed a job, which he knew, would bring caustic comments from Rusty and Peter.

From the kitchen came the sound of crockery and he resisted an impulse to go and speak to Anne. Bodily weariness had blunted the edge of his unhappiness, and as he turned to go to the homestead he wondered if, when he was more rested, he would be able to review everything calmly and dispassionately. He still loved Anne and would always do so, no matter what she had done or what she would do in the future. It was the thought of her deception which still hurt.

"Oh, there you are," Mrs. Smythe broke into his thoughts as she came on to the verandah and stopped beside him. "Joy is in bed. She was tired, poor child, and she wants to say good-night."

Pat sighed and went with her into the hall, hesitating in the doorway of Anne's room. Joy called to him imperiously.

"Where have you been all this time? And where's Anne?"

"I don't think we need bother her tonight, Joy."

"I want her," she pouted, her eyes downcast. "She *always* says goodnight."

Her uncle looked at her face and rose from the bed. All of them were trying to keep the child's mind off the raging flood waters, they did not wish her to be frightened by the thought that she could not return home to her mother for quite a long time. He returned to the kitchen where Anne was standing by the sink, her hands in the soapy water, and Roddie, drooping a little, was awkwardly drying up.

"Miss Smith."

"Yes, Mr. Kennedy?" she turned with a smile at the old familiar greeting.

"Joy insists on saying goodnight," he said stiffly. "Do you mind coming over?"

"Of course not!" She dried her hands swiftly, flung her apron over the back of a chair and without a glance in Roddie's direction, went to the door. She paused by Pat's side and in the swift glance they gave each other both realised how tired the other was.

"How's the river?" she asked quietly as they moved side by side along the path.

"Nearly up to the top of the wall."

"I'll have a look at it later. Do you think it will hold?"

"It'll have to!" Pat stuck out his jaw, as though the idea of the wall he had planned around the station failing at the crucial moment was impossible. "Come on, it's time Joy was asleep."

The little girl smiled at the sight of them coming into the room together and put out her hands to draw them down to her. They sat on either side of the bed, remote but very conscious of each other's nearness.

"Three faces, one kiss," announced Joy.

"What on earth do you mean?" asked her uncle.

"That's what Daddy and Mummy used to do," she explained. "We all kissed each other at the same time." She saw the gathering of his heavy eyebrows and her lips quivered. "Daddy's in the Islands and Mummy's in town and I've no one but you and Anne to kiss me," she cried with a rush, blinking her eyes and causing Anne to bend her head quickly to hide a smile. "Well?" she asked impatiently.

"All right," snapped Pat.

"Anne?"

"Yes," she agreed, raising her head. Joy's lips touched her lightly and drew away, leaving the other two faces almost touching each other. For a moment the grey eyes stared into the brown, Anne was aware of a pulse throbbing in her throat and her hand moved swiftly to his shoulder as though to steady herself.

"Oh, curse you, woman!" he muttered, and gave her a quick hard kiss. Without another word or a backward glance he went from the room and Joy and Anne looked at each other.

"Did you mind being cursed?" asked Joy with interest.

Anne's eyes were shining. "No. But I could spank you!"

"Are you going to?"

"Not tonight." She hugged the child's slender body to her. "Tomorrow perhaps, if you're naughty!"

Joy chuckled, and well satisfied with her strategy slid down under the one sheet and said goodnight.

Pat did not reappear that evening, which was understandable. ⸱ sought the comfort of his bed and was not at all pleased ⸱ n Mr. Jeen determined to have his revenge for the way he had been worked throughout the long day, knocked loudly on his door with his plastered hands and demanded the key of the office.

"I'm going to start on the books," he announced pompously when Pat, bleary-eyed, opened the door.

"Tonight?"

"Why not? The sooner the better. Then Miss Carrington-Smythe will know exactly how she stands."

Pat glowered at him. "There's time enough for the books. You'll be here for a long time yet."

"A fact you've pointed out to me on numerous occasions today. You've been busy, perhaps when you aren't quite so busy you might decide to go through the books again and alter figures in another way now you know we are here to check up –"

"Why, you –"

"Steady, Kennedy!" he cried sharply, drawing back well out of Pat's reach. "We know what you've been doing all this time. I'm going to make a start. There is nothing else to do here, the newspapers are old ones, we read them in Sydney days ago. Also," he held out his hands, "I refuse to assist in any way whatsoever with a shovel tomorrow or any other day. Look at my hands!"

Pat looked and the elusive little grin passed over his lips. "You're soft," he remarked.

"I'm not a navvy," cried Mr. Jeen, incensed.

"Strangely enough, neither am I," retorted the other mildly. "Here's the key, seeing you're so insistent, and – Good hunting!"

The solicitor stared at the key in his hands, then at the closed door. Turning quickly he winced at the pain which shot from his shoulders and wished devoutly that he was back in Sydney in the luxurious comfort of his own home.

Unlocking the office door, Mr. Jeen switched on the light and his expression changed. He had been hoping for such an opportunity; his partner's cold and sore throat was a blessing in disguise, for there were the books and here was his chance to prove without doubt that Pat Kennedy was nothing but a common thief. There would be no doubts about it when he had finished, he thought. Happily he sat down and surveyed the desk, blissfully unaware that only a few hours previously Miss Carrington-Smythe had been seated at the same desk, glancing hurriedly through the same books.

Blistered hands and aching shoulders were forgotten as the solicitor warmed to his task. One book after another was carefully scrutinised and the column of figures on a separate piece of paper became longer. Mr. Jeen began to frown, he lifted his head and his lips moved as he reckoned up amounts in his head. But a scuffling sound distracted his attention, there was a shout from somewhere in the darkness and he jumped to his feet as something moved on the verandah outside the office.

"What now?" he asked impatiently, going to the french windows and peeped out. A woolly head met his, and with a cry of fright Mr. Jeen drew back and slammed the window shut.

"Head them round this way," cried a voice in the garden.

Everyone sounded to be running up and down the verandahs and amid the shouts and barking of dogs came the frightened bleating of sheep. Some of them in the paddock near the homestead had panicked for an unknown reason and the leaders, having found the garden gate open, had rushed across the lawns towards the house. There they panicked still further and two even managed to get into the kitchen in their fright, where they were met by Mrs. Smythe waving a broom. Pat, half-drugged with sleep, staggered to the window and demanded to know if the world had gone mad. Upon being informed what had transpired he lost his temper with Rusty, who was the nearest to him, and the groom, angered by this unreasonableness, immediately began to shout back.

As she heard them, Mrs. Smythe leaned on the broom and

started to laugh. This enforced isolation was bringing everyone's faults to the fore, little things which could have been humorous assumed an air of tragedy, tempers were becoming frayed and patience no longer existed unless it remained in Mr. Norton's heart. Even Dick, paddling round the grass in his pyjamas, was swearing at Jan for having awakened him. Rounding sheep in the garden of Gum Valley at eleven o'clock was not his idea of pleasure, he stated forcibly. Things sounded to be getting out of hand, Rusty was now arguing with Peter, and Alan could be heard invoking evil on whoever left the gate open. Then Pat arrived and took charge and within five minutes things began to be sorted out, the sheep were being moved in a sedate file back out of the garden and by the aid of hurricane lamps Jan and the groom were repairing the netting fence which had been broken by sheer force of numbers. Mr. Jeen and Roddie were absent; both considered it to their advantage if they feigned sleep.

Pat became aware of someone working beside him. From beneath the hem of a light coat he glimpsed the delicate pink of a nightdress and raised his head to meet Anne's laughing eyes.

"What next?" she asked.

"God only knows! And why aren't you in bed? You shouldn't be parading out here in your nightdress when all the men are about."

"They've been so busy they haven't noticed me," she replied. "Mother has prepared a drink, Pat, it's ready now."

He tried to remember that he was still annoyed with her, but the thought of a drink of tea proved too attractive, and after making sure all the sheep had left the garden and that the gate and the fence were secure once more he went into the small sitting-room where Mrs. Smythe was sitting behind the teapot and Anne was curled up in her favourite position on the settee.

"I thought this might help you to get to sleep quicker," said

Mrs. Smythe comfortably. "You've had so many disturbances — I hope there aren't any more." She passed his cup and Pat subsided into his usual chair with a sigh of thankfulness. In the silence that followed the roar of the flood water could be plainly heard and they listened in silence.

"How long does it take to go down, once it starts dropping?" asked Anne.

"A great deal depends upon how the water is getting away further down," answered Pat. "Two or three towns have built levees to prevent the streets being flooded, if by any ill-chance one of the levees broke the water would naturally spread out quicker and it would reduce the volume which is being built up."

"There must be millions and millions of gallons of water rushing over the countryside," murmured Mrs. Smythe thoughtfully. "And most of it going to waste. Will it make any difference to your plans for the future?"

"I have no plans —" he began awkwardly, and stopped as Anne looked at him. He stirred his tea, sipped it and glanced at her out of the corners of his eyes. She was watching him anxiously and there was pleading in her tired face.

"No plans?" asked her mother, looking very surprised and delightfully innocent. "I always imagined you country folk had hundreds of plans which were dependent on the weather for their execution. Ploughing, sowing, harvesting, such things you know." She smiled at him warmly and encouragingly.

"It will delay the ploughing," he muttered, wishing she would go to bed and leave him alone with Anne. He felt in the mood for an argument, which might clear the air between them, also he wanted an explanation of Roddie's behaviour on the night of his arrival.

"And will it spoil the land?" she went on enquiringly.

Pat looked down at his empty cup before answering. "No. In the long run it will improve it," he said slowly. "When the water subsides it will leave behind it a layer of silt, which will smell like nothing on earth, and after that is poughed in we should get better crops. The silt is really fine topsoil which has been washed downstream."

"So one man's loss is another man's gain," said Anne thoughtfully, and he nodded. "I understand."

Her mother looked at her and noticed the drooping shoulders beneath the light coat Anne was still wearing over her nightdress.

"Pet, you're tired. And Pat is too. So off to bed, both of you. No, leave these things, I'll attend to them, for I've done very little today, despite all appearances to the contrary. Maybe when we wake up we shall find the river has started to drop."

"I wish I could hope so," said Pat, getting to his feet and stretching, at the same time yawning loudly. "But you don't know this river, Mrs. Smythe. It twists for so many miles and is fed by so many creeks and smaller rivers. All that water has yet to pass here and I can't see any of us being able to leave for another week or so."

"Are you particularly worried about the thought?" she asked.

He dropped his arms and looked at Anne. "No," he answered slowly, still gazing at the girl's face. "For myself I'm not worried."

"Pat," she leaned forward and spoke in a whisper, "does that mean you have changed your mind about leaving?"

He smiled slightly. "I did not say so."

"But you won't go, will you?" she pleaded urgently, forgetting her mother, who was watching them both with tender eyes. "You'll stay?"

"A great deal depends on Mr. Maynard," he said softly. "I might not have any choice in the matter by the time he's completed auditing the books."

Anne seemed to droop even more against the cushions.

"I'd forgotten that," she murmured. "Yes, I'd completely forgotten Mr. Maynard. And Mr. Jeen," she added beneath her breath.

CHAPTER NINE

MRS. SMYTHE went to her room humming to herself. She had the feeling that all was going to be well for her daughter and the man she had chosen to share her life. Pat had recovered from the blow he had received when he learned Anne's identity and because of his interest in Gum Valley they would settle to a placid existence out here in the bush. True, there was still Mr. Maynard to be dealt with and the matter of the altered accounts, but if it could be proved that all the money had been used solely on the station Mrs. Smythe could not see that there would be much difficulty in straightening things out.

She settled herself on her bed, but sleep eluded her, and she lay in the darkness for a long time listening to Barbara's quiet breathing and thinking over her previous visits to Gum Valley. Gradually her eyelids closed, but she only dozed and was awake immediately there came a whimper from the other bed.

"Mrs. Smythe," whispered Barbara urgently. "Are you awake?" Her voice was trembling with fear.

"Yes, dear. Wide awake," said the other calmly.

"Can you hear that gurgling noise?"

"I can."

"What is it? Put the light on, please! Oh, it sounds so queer!"

It did sound queer, thought Mrs. Smythe as she walked across the room to the light switch, like a hundred children blowing bubbles under the carpet. The next minute she changed her mind. The noise sounded more like water gurgling away from the bath after the plug had been released.

"No light," she murmured, moving the switch up and down, and Barbara, hearing the faint clicks, shuddered and clutched the sheets with her hands.

"What's the matter? Why won't the lights go on? It's so dark, I'm frightened. I wish I hadn't come out here!"

"I have a torch somewhere," the other voice came placidly from the far side of the room. "There's no need for alarm, Barbara, possibly the batteries have run down or something has gone wrong with the switch. I once stayed in a hotel where the switches were temperamental —"

"But the gurgling noise?" Barbara's voice rose sharply. She could understand the lights going wrong, they even did that in the city, but this other noise was unexplainable.

"Ah! I've found it," cried Mrs. Smythe triumphantly and a golden beam shot across the room and hesitated on the girl's white frightened face. Then it swept down on to the carpeted floor and went round in circles. "Nothing in here to alarm you, child. I'll peep out of the window, perhaps the sheep have come back and one might be under the house."

Pulling aside the heavy curtains, Mrs. Smythe switched off her torch and peered outside. The torch was unnecessary as the whole garden was bathed in brilliant moonlight. Looking round she caught her breath and stiffened. The retainer wall which had so laboriously been erected had evidently collapsed under the strain of holding back the river and now the water was rushing down the paths and over the lawns. The gurgling noises from the house were being caused by countless air holes being filled. Soon those would fill up and the muddy water would be inches deep under Gum Valley.

Barbara, watching her intently, had seen her draw herself up and she scrambled from her bed to rush to her side. At the sight of the water running beneath the window she immediately screamed and a cool hand was placed over her mouth.

"Do you want to wake up the whole household?" cried the other sharply. "Be quiet, Barbara! Do you hear me?"

Wide-eyed, the girl nodded, and Mrs. Smythe removed her hand, at the same time watching her intently.

"Don't have a fit of hysterics," she warned, "or I shall do something drastic."

"That's the river!" cried Barbara, pointing with trembling fingers. "It's here – under the house and round it! Oh, what shall we do? Wake up that jackaroo and tell him to do something. He seems to know all the answers, he must get out of bed and get us out of here! We'll drown!"

"Fiddlesticks! We might get very wet and be very uncomfortable, but we shan't drown." Her voice was very matter-of-fact. "And as for waking Pat, I shall do no such thing. He's tired out and needs his rest and he can do nothing about this lot at all. Oh, yes, I know he's in charge here," she said hurriedly as Barbara opened her mouth. "But he's no Canute and neither he nor anyone else can push the water back through the broken wall. My dear," she said impressively, "you're witnessing a miracle of Nature, something you might never see again in your lifetime –"

"I certainly *don't* want to see anything like it again," whispered Barbara, who was trembling from head to foot. "It's horrible, and I wish I was back in Sydney." She began to cry in earnest and Mrs. Smythe put her arms round the shaking shoulders.

"Come back to bed. There's nothing we can do. Even if we got everyone out we should merely sit around and wait until morning and as a result be bad-tempered through missing our sleep. So we might just as well be comfortable until daylight."

She shepherded Barbara into her own bed, cradled her in her arms as she used to do with Anne when she was small and talked soothingly until she felt the trembling body relax against her. For herself she had no fear, she was confident the foundations of Gum Valley would withstand this rush of water. If they didn't – well, she would simply do as she was told by the jackaroo and hope for the best. Once the first rush of the flowing water had passed it would rise slowly and gently as the river rose still higher, there would be no great depth and it should be possible to paddle round the place. They had food and plenty of clothing, what else did they need? she asked herself sleepily. Others were in a far worse predicament down the river's length, and with that thought uppermost in her mind Mrs. Smythe finally drifted off to sleep.

One by one the others went on to the verandah in the morning and surveyed in silence the muddy water which surrounded them. Pat looked at it with heavy eyes and compressed lips. He had done his best, but the river had beaten him. Upon investigation he discovered that the retainer wall had been trampled upon by the sheep the previous evening. They had slipped and stumbled over its whole length, they had jostled each other along its flat top and so weakened it, and the water, backed by the swiftly-flowing river, had seeped through gradually and then broken it with a rush.

Anne, watching his face, said nothing. This was not the time for words and she realised it. Somehow she supplied a hot tasty breakfast, and as Pat sat down before a plateful of chops and eggs, with a steaming cup of tea at his elbow, he gave her a grateful glance. Anne immediately responded with a smile, and the day, despite the surrounding flood waters, felt brighter for both of them.

During the morning an attempt was made to block up the

breaks in the retainer wall; some held and so reduced the volume of water which poured across the lawns and lessened the danger to the house foundations. Breaks were also made in the thick hedges to let the water run more freely away from the house, and up to their knees in slime, Pat and the others tried to dig trenches further from the homestead to guide the streams into nearby paddocks. Overhead the sky was a deep blue and there was not a cloud to be seen, the sun was hot and dazzling and very soon perspiration ran down each grimy face.

"We can do no more," announced Pat, going to the verandah and glancing at each face in turn. "Except wait for the river to drop. Did you hear anything on the radio this morning?"

"The battery is flat," said Anne, "and we can't re-charge it because water has got into the electricity plant."

"So that's that!" he nodded. "For a week nobody will know of our plight and if anything drastic happens in the world we shall be in total ignorance of the fact."

He screwed up his eyes against the sun's glare and looked towards the main stream of the river, where logs and trees were rushing down, brushing against the remaining gum trees or catching in the huge forks and making a barrier where more debris, brushwood and shrubs, piled up in untidy heaps. Dick was now perched upon the top of a fence with a rifle in his hands, taking shots at anything he saw moving, maybe a rabbit or a snake caught on a log in the treacherous current.

Rusty decided to spend his day of leisure in bed. There was nothing for any of them to do until the water began to subside and he had a lot of leeway to make up as regards sleep. Rather balefully he lay with his hands behind his head, staring at the blank wall before him, planning his future, for he fully intended leaving Gum Valley as soon as it was possible. His attitude had changed the most since he had been told who Anne really was. She was no longer a cook but one of the Bosses, a race apart, one of the moneyed people, and he felt resentful that she should have allowed him to be so attentive to her. He was a groom, a man who milked cows and killed sheep for meat, he was a hard-working bloke, he told himself, and had nothing at all in common with Anne Carrington-Smythe. There were other properties, places more accessible to town, away from river banks.

Roddie walked through the house with his hands in his pockets, at a loss as to what to do with himself. For a while he thumped on the piano, then Mr. Jeen snarled at him to be quiet, the noise was getting on his nerves, and he closed the piano lid with a bang and wandered on to the verandah. There was nothing to read, for the books and papers were old ones, he could not fiddle with his car, for that was standing outside the garden gate in a foot of water, and he was not going to offer to help the jackaroo with whatever he was doing in one of the store sheds. Anne was busy in the hot kitchen and Mr. Norton was with her; there was nowhere, he thought crossly, where he could be alone. Even his bed was in a public spot on the verandah. Roddie began to feel oppressed at the sight of the wet countryside. There was water everywhere, blue in the distance and a muddy brown near at hand.

Anne was the only one who really worked throughout the long day. She had plenty to occupy her time and it was not until the evening when everyone had been fed and the dishes washed and put away that she could relax. Curled up on the settee, with her mother sitting at the other end, she glanced at the people in the room, there was Barbara, still very silent and looking pinched around the mouth; Roddie sprawled with his legs over the arm of a chair, yawning discreetly behind his hand, and the two solicitors bent together over sheets of paper. Anne frowned as she watched them, for Mr. Maynard had stated, barely an hour before, that in the morning he intended to have a showdown with the jackaroo, Mr. Jeen had completed his job with the books and it was his duty, therefore, to place the full facts before Miss Carrington-Smythe.

Pat was missing and she hoped he was asleep. She thought of him longingly. Whatever he had done and no matter what the consequences as a result of his actions, she would stand by him. In fact, she thought, looking at Mr. Maynard sombrely, she would refuse to take any action at all against her unpaid manager. If only the river would drop and enable these people to leave and so give Pat and herself a little privacy and time to say that which had to be said. If she could convince him once and for all that her whole happiness depended upon him staying at Gum Valley with her, he might then ask her to marry him, and once she was his wife he would be safe from any prosecution.

Mr. Jeen disappeared, and one by one the others said goodnight and left the room, Mrs. Smythe going with Barbara, leaving Anne alone. For a long time she sat with her eyes closed, thinking of her life in Sydney, of her flat and the yacht moored in Rose Bay, deliberately bringing pictures into her mind, yet not one excited her. There was nothing to call her back, the Anne who had lived there and who had travelled the world over was not the Anne sitting in the old-fashioned room at Gum Valley. She felt they were two different people. One had existed, the other was living.

Carefully she lowered the flame in the oil lamp, which had been unearthed from some half-forgotten corner to help them in the emergency, and blew out the light. Feeling her way carefully through the room she went into the hall and then on to the verandah. Roddie was asleep and did not move as she slipped silently past his bed. After gazing at the garden for a while she turned to go back into the house, when a flickering light from the office window caught her eye, and curious to see what Mr. Jeen was doing in there when everyone else had gone to bed, Anne crept along until she was beneath the lighted window. To her chagrin she could see nothing, and as she had no desire to raise her head up against the glass, she glanced round for a better vantage point. The only one was on top of the retainer wall; without hesitation she slipped off her shoes, lifted her dress and stepped down into the water.

From the top of the slippery wall it was possible to see the office, as much of it as was lit by the single lamp, and as she watched, Anne's face became puzzled. What was he doing in there? Mr. Jeen was busy tearing up papers and placing the scraps in a white flour bag, obviously for disposal later. He looked exceptionally pleased with himself too, and clinging to her precarious perch, the girl waited, her head buzzing with sudden ideas. She shifted her position the better to make herself comfortable. The soil was wet and slimy beneath her, but the night was warm and there was little chance of catching cold.

For ten minutes she sat motionless, watching the solicitor's busy hands, then she drew in her breath sharply as he proceeded to tear cheque butts into shreds. Now there was no doubt at all in her mind as to who was the real culprit. The man who had taken most of the revenue from Gum Valley and who had caused a great deal of heartache was seated in the office chair, destroying evidence which could prove Pat had spoken the truth. Thankful she had obeyed a strange intuition and written down for herself most of the figures in the books, a wild anger against the solicitor filled the girl's heart and her eyes clouded over. She had doubted Pat only for a little while, it was true, nevertheless, she *had* wondered if he had been feathering his nest at her expense. No wonder the property had been going downhill and the jackaroo had had such a struggle to get anything. The unscrupulous solicitor had been systematically robbing her for years.

"And I, with my lack of interest in the place, made it so easy for him and so difficult for Pat," she thought miserably. "It's all my own fault. Oh, my darling, I'm sorry. We certainly will have a showdown tomorrow, but it won't be you who is exposed as a thief, it will be the man in there who looks so very pleased with himself! I shall have to stay here until he's finished and then follow him to see where he puts the bag. I must have it, it's essential, for without it Mr. Maynard will never believe me."

Mr. Jeen wondered if he had seen something move along the wall outside, and for a few moments he thought it was another sheep; from beneath his heavy lids he kept glancing into the darkness and knew beyond doubt that the thing crouching out there was not a four-footed animal. Someone was on the retainer wall, someone who had not been there before. The outline was light-coloured but blurred by the gauze netting which screened the windows. Lazily he stood up as though he had completed his task, placed the last of the scraps of paper in the small bag and turned off the lamp. Immediately his eyes moved quickly towards the thing which was now very definitely groping along the wall, and leaving the bag on the table to be collected later he moved quietly to the French windows, and after opening them, slipped silently on to the verandah, his heart pounding uncomfortably. Someone had been watching him and had seen all he had been doing, and he was determined that that person, no matter who it was, was not going to expose him. The last few years had been profitable and regrettably they had come to an end. He remembered the anger and horror with which he had heard that Miss Carrington-Smythe had gone to Gum Valley. Until now he had been clever enough to cover his tracks and during the past two days, alone in his office, he had snatched the chance of throwing the entire blame on to someone else, a man who had already committed himself by confessing that he had altered the accounts. It had been very easy, he had felt perfectly secure, and his security was not going to be spoilt at the last minute by some prowler.

The figure in the shadows was in difficulties. As he crept closer he could hear quickened breathing and the sound of tearing material. His hands went out and Anne recoiled, almost losing her balance. Behind her on the far side of the wall the water was about six feet deep. It was well in the shadows and in the quick glance she threw in that direction it looked evil and dark. She moved and a shaft of moonlight fell on her face, causing Mr. Jeen to gasp.

"You!"

"It's me, all right," she agreed, still pulling at her skirt which had become entangled in one of the shrubs.

"What are you doing here?" he hissed in her ear. "Spying on me?"

"I was," admitted Anne almost cheerfully, and the next moment a heavy blow on the side of her face made her slip backwards.

Mr. Jeen lost his head and became panic-stricken. The blow had been struck in a sudden fit of savage fury, and as the girl fell to the far side of the wall he realised that he had done the worst possible thing, for by hitting her he had confessed to all he had been doing and made his own position more insecure than ever. From past recollections of Miss Carrington-Smythe he knew she might, after some persuasion, forgive him the thefts over the years, but never would she forgive him for laying hands upon her person. At all costs she must be silenced, and he continued to strike out viciously with his fists.

Anne gave a faint cry, clutched the wall vainly with wet, muddy hands as she tried to dodge the blows, and finally slipped right back into the water. Mud choked her nose and mouth and prevented her crying out, and she kicked despairingly away from the wall and those cruel stinging hands. Mr. Jeen leaned over to watch, he saw her head appear and disappear and waited with horror in his eyes to see what would happen. He did not know whether to feel sorry or glad when Anne did not come into his sight again, and after peering for ten minutes into the shadows and moonlit patches of water he turned away, his finer instincts urging him to seek help to find the girl, and the instinct of self-preservation urging him to keep quiet about what had happened. "No one will ever know," he kept telling himself. "No one has seen us. No one can now prove that Kennedy hasn't taken all the money from Gum Valley. I'm safe, I'm safe."

With many a backward glance, he moved quietly to the room he shared with Mr. Maynard, made sure his partner was still sleeping soundly and removed his wet shoes and socks.

Half-stunned from the blows she had received, Anne swam slowly away from the house. Her legs became entangled in the branches of a submerged fruit tree, and as the twigs scratched her skin, she kicked out angrily – no tree was going to impede her progress. The slight current carried her along parallel with the retainer wall and she could see the roof and chimneys of the homestead silhouetted against the sky. More twigs scratched her legs, and half in wonder she realised she was swimming above the orchard; if ever she got out of here and solicitors and jackaroos enabled her to live in peace at Gum Valley, she would one day look at these trees from ground level and wonder at herself for being able to swim above them.

The roar of the river from over the flooded paddock sounded nearer and her labouring heart gave a lurch. If she drifted into the main current she would never come out alive and Pat and her mother would be left to worry and wonder for the rest of their lives as to what had become of her or why she had fallen into the river when she should have been in bed.

"No river," she said grimly, and was cheered at the sound of her own voice, "and certainly not Mr. Jeen, is going to prevent me from telling the world all I know!" and she kicked the harder, making for a break in the wall on the far side of the men's quarters. The thought of exposing the solicitor and of clearing Pat's name spurred her on, it gave her just the little extra effort and courage to enable her to finally get her hands into the mud and heave herself out of the water. But the effort all but exhausted her and she half-crawled through the shallow water in the small paddock where normally Rusty milked the cows towards the store sheds.

Anne knew she was going to faint, and dimly she realised that if she fainted out here her face would fall in the slime and she would drown. Pushing open the store shed door, she fell on the floor, crawled painfully into the darkness and fainted from sheer shock when she bumped into some cases and they fell around her with a tremendous clatter.

Joy had been dreaming. At first it was a pleasant dream and she was enjoying it, for Uncle Pat was rowing the battered tub along the track towards Murra Creek and he was making her laugh as he guided their boat round trees and cattle. But somehow Uncle Pat fell out and the tub bobbed into mid-stream, she was alone and was being carried rapidly away from Gum Valley. It had started to rain again and away in the distance she could see Jan waving farewell from the top of the retainer wall. Joy stood up in the tub and shouted at the top of her voice. Wet with perspiration and fright, she continued to shout as the tub began to sink beneath her and her voice rose higher in her panic.

"You're all right, Joy," cried a soothing voice, and her eyes opened.

In the light of a flickering candle she stared up into Mrs. Smythe's face and her small body quivered.

"Oh !"

The candlelight wavered as it was moved to enable Mrs. Smythe to lift the child in her arms. "You must have been dreaming."

"I was." Joy cast a swift glance around the room to make sure it was there and that she was not on the river in a sinking tub and then buried her face against Mrs. Smythe's shoulder. "All about the bathtub."

"You must forget it, for it wasn't true, whatever it was. You're all right now, for look, you're in your own little bed," Mrs. Smythe consoled her, and wondered wildly why Anne was not in bed at two o'clock in the morning. The bed had not been slept in either.

"Where's Anne?" Joy was calming down.

"She hasn't come to bed yet, dear. Shall I leave the candle for you?"

The child looked up shyly. "No, for if Teddy ever hears I had to have a light in my room he would always be teasing me about it. Give me my doll and leave the door open. If Anne hurries I'll keep awake until she comes."

"All right," Mrs. Smythe smiled, a kiss was lightly dropped on the little girl's forehead and the curtains were pulled back so the moonlight could flood the room. "There, that makes it lighter for you and no one can tease you about it! You won't dream any more, will you?"

"I'll try not to," promised Joy, half sitting up and feeling much braver now the room was not dark.

Once out in the hall, Mrs. Smythe ran as quickly as she could with the candle into each of the sitting rooms, into the dining room, kitchen, office, billiard-room, she ran into every room barring the one the solicitors shared. But there was no sign of her daughter. Hurriedly she glanced at the clock again. It was turned two and something must be wrong, so without hesitation she opened the door of Pat's room, fumbled for a moment with the switch before remembering it would not work and crossed to his side to wake him.

"Wake up, Pat," she said in a low voice. "Wake up immediately!"

It was only afterwards that Mrs. Smythe could smile at the startled expression on his face as he grunted, half turned over and opened his eyes to blink at the sight of the greying head swathed in a black hairnet bending over his bed.

"What on earth – ?" he began impatiently.

"Anne's missing," she stated without preamble. "It's turned two and her bed hasn't been slept in." He was wide awake now, sitting up and staring at her. "Joy was shouting and screaming in her sleep, I went in wondering why Anne hadn't quietened her and found the child alone."

He swung his legs out from under the sheet. "I'll get dressed."

In the hall Mrs. Smythe waited, experiencing again the peculiar feeling in her stomach which had always appeared when years ago, Anne had been missing from her usual place in the garden. She tried reminding herself that always her daughter had been nearby, sometimes hiding in a fit of mischief and deaf to all entreaties to come out, sometimes merely lost in a game of her own. Though the little Anne was now a grown woman and had lived alone, travelled alone and flown alone for a long time, her mother thought of the river and felt weak and sick.

"Steady," said a low voice at her elbow as she leaned back against the wall.

"I've been in every room," said Mrs. Smythe, pulling herself together quickly, for the tall figure by her side gave her a feeling of great confidence. Whatever had happened to Anne or wherever she was, Pat would find her. "Excepting Mr. Maynard's. And I can't think she'll be in there," she added crossly, and he grinned.

"I'll have a look round. No need to wake anyone else yet." He propelled her towards the sitting room. "Light the lamps and put the kettle on the Primus, Anne may be wet or cold and will want a drink and a wash."

He sounded unworried, but as the candlelight flickered on his face she could see the expression in his eyes. Then he was gone, and she had the hard unthankful task of merely waiting until he returned.

Swiftly Pat went through the house to satisfy himself that Anne was not here, then splashed his way across to the kitchen. That was in darkness and he struck a match, peering round by the light of the tiny flame. The kitchen was empty, as was the men's dining-room. All the other rooms were in total darkness too, even Mr. Norton was asleep. His heart began to thump queerly and his thoughts as he stared round the moonlit waters on the garden were troubled and unhappy. What had Anne been doing? When he had last seen her she had been curled up in the corner of the settee, talking to her mother and her guests, she had smiled, that little intimate smile she kept for him alone when he had paused to say goodnight. What would she do after everyone had gone to bed? The natural answer to that question, he thought with a worried frown, would be for her to go to her room and go to sleep in the bed beside that of Joy. He could think of no reason why she should suddenly decide to leave the house. Wherever she went there was water. Not enough to drown in around the house, he added quickly, and Anne had too much sense to start trapesing along the retainer wall in the middle of the night.

Methodically he began to paddle over the lawns and round the garden. From there he went round the men's quarters and back to the kitchen. With his mouth set in a thin line he glanced towards the river. That was a foolish thought, Anne could not be there, she must be somewhere round the house, she *must*. His wandering glance took in the store sheds; he would look in there and if there was no sign of her he would return to the house and awaken Roddie and the others from their deep unconcerned slumber, rouse the men and go over every inch of the ground. If necessary, he would tear Gum Valley to pieces in his attempts to find her.

For one wild moment he wondered if she had so taken their quarrel and his bitterness to heart that she had taken a certain way out of her difficulties, then he scoffed at the idea. Anne had too much courage to ever do such a thing. He would not think of the river again; it was something too horrible for words to think of his Anne drifting away on that ferocious current.

Hesitating in the half open doorway of the shed, he struck another match, immediately there was a faint thankful cry of "Pat!"

"Anne – oh, thank God you're here," he cried, striding inside. "Where are you, darling? Are you all right?"

"No," answered Anne frankly from the darkness, "I'm not."

Dizzy with relief because he had found her, Pat laughed softly at her reply.

"I'm here, under some cases," she went on, trying to keep her voice steady. "Oh, Pat, how thankful I am you've come!"

Another match flickered and by its feeble light he glimpsed her lying on the floor with three heavy cases pinning one leg to the boards. Instantly he was at her side. Anne felt his hands move caressingly over her face and she pulled them away as she turned round, and as his lips met hers she knew he would never leave her alone at Gum Valley. Despite her position and the pain she had endured during the past three hours, her heart sang with relief and gladness.

"Oh, Anne," Pat breathed her name again and again, "I thought I'd lost you. I've searched everywhere, if anything had happened to you I think I should have died too." He buried his face in her hair and tightened his arms, holding her close and murmuring in her ear. "Anne, my lovely Anne. But, sweet, why the store shed?"

"Because –" she started to explain, but completely lost the thread of what she was going to say as he kissed her again. Then, against her will, as he moved her in his arms she moaned, "My leg!"

With a muttered word of apology he let her go and felt with gentle fingers from her knee to her ankle. One of the cases had splintered in its fall and a long sliver of wood was sticking into the soft flesh.

"I've tried every way to move it," she gasped, hanging desperately on to his shoulders for the comfort of his nearness. "But there was another case behind it, because I was pinned down I couldn't twist round sufficiently to lift it. If you'd stowed the cases in a proper manner in the first place they wouldn't have fallen down when I bumped against them!" she cried accusingly, on the verge of tears, still gripping his shoulder. She was fighting hard to gain control of her feelings, but the exhausting and frightening swim, followed by the blackness which had enveloped her when she fell on the store room floor and the long wait in the terrifying darkness had almost taken her nerve. On top of that was the overwhelming relief in the knowledge that Pat still loved her and had forgiven her for all that had happened. Too much had happened all at once.

He was smiling as he lifted a case. "How long have you been here?"

"I don't know. Ages. And it's been awful with only Sammy to keep me company –"

"Sammy?" he breathed, standing perfectly still. "*Sammy?*"

"Yes," Anne nodded, and wondered at the urgency with which he bent down to continue his task and the cases were pushed hurriedly on one side. "He slithered past me in the darkness, I nearly screamed. But I didn't," she added proudly. "He's still about somewhere. Oh, Pat," her voice broke oddly, "if I ever marry you you'll have to get rid of this snake. It annoys me!"

"*If* you ever marry me? You're darn well going to!"

"Oh! Am I?" She sounded surprised, then gave a huge sigh of thankfulness when the last of the weight was removed from her leg. Gingerly her hand moved over the swollen flesh; it felt slightly sticky to the touch and she wondered if the wound was a deep one. A memory of the iodine bottle flashed through her mind and she cringed at the thought. "I thought I should be here all night," she confessed as he lifted her gently and carried her towards the open door. "I shouted, but with the roar of the water I knew no one would hear me." Against her face, his felt damp. "Why, you're perspiring! Am I so heavy?"

Pat shook his head. "Not at all, this is one job I like doing! But you'll perspire too when I tell you that I removed Sammy from the store shed when the floods began."

"You mean – it was another snake?" she whispered, horrified.

"It must have been. Sammy is in the shed where I keep my car."

"Pat, I'm sure I'm going to cry!"

"There's no need to, darling, not now. Oh, Anne, oh – don't!"

She gave in to her feelings at last. The thought of the unknown snake sliding over the shed floor was too much for her and she lay with her head on his shoulder and wept without restraint. Pat glanced down at her rather helplessly and remembered her mother waiting alone in the house. She would know what to do with her daughter, and he waded quickly through the water past the men's rooms and the kitchen and through the gate to the house. This was the first time he had seen Anne upset. Her surrender to her emotions filled him with compassion, for he knew the strain of whatever had happened must have been terrific to break her nerve. If she thought her tears would remind him of Barbara she was very much mistaken; these were the tears of an overwrought woman, not the tears of a nerveless girl.

Mrs. Smythe was on the verandah and when she saw Pat coming across the garden in the moonlight with a bedraggled-looking Anne in his arms and heard his voice, amazingly soft and gentle, the tenseness left her body and she drew a quivering breath. For a moment her eyes met his imploringly and he smiled.

"She was sitting in the storeroom of all places!" he cried, looking down at the girl's face. "Why, sweet, you're all muddy!"

"I don't feel at all glamorous or beautiful at the moment," Anne sniffed through her tears. "I'm plastered in mud! But," she added with a flash of her old fire, "you've mud on your face as well, Mr. Kennedy!"

"That's because I've just kissed you, Miss Smith," he retorted, and Mrs. Smythe laughed happily and thankfully.

She helped Anne undress and tenderly bathed the tired body with all the warm water she had, her hands lingering over a task she had not performed for many years. Not a question did she ask either as she looked with horror at the swollen bleeding leg, and as Anne followed her glance she shuddered.

"Don't let Pat pour iodine into that!" she cried. "It would be the last straw. I couldn't stand it, Mother."

"Indeed no!" answered Mrs. Smythe placidly. "I've ointment and all kinds of what-nots in one of my cases, I always carry them, for I seem to land myself in some peculiar places and one never knows when they will be needed. I'll get Pat to carry you back into the sitting room and while we're having a drink of tea you can tell us how you came to be in a store shed plastered with mud at this time in the morning!"

"I can walk," protested Anne, as her mother went to the door to call Pat.

"I'm sure he'll be only too pleased to do as I ask, pet," said her mother, unperturbed. "What was it you asked me to look for in the office? A flour bag? Why put such things in there, pray?"

Comfortable and relaxed on the settee, with the injured leg bandaged and soothed, with cushions behind her head and with the precious flour bag on her lap, Anne told them what had happened to her since they had said goodnight and left her the previous evening. As they listened Mrs. Smythe's face went white, but Pat flushed a vivid red and he started to his feet.

"I'll kill him for this!" he cried, striding towards the door, and the girl struggled to her feet.

"You'll do no such thing! Pat –"

"He hit you!" he snapped. "He hurt you, because of him you might have drowned."

"But I wasn't." She was looking at him with soft brown eyes, filled with delight at his concern for her welfare. "Come back, dear. I'm going to deal with this and I have the proof," she indicated the flour bag. "Mr. Maynard said he would have a showdown and we will, although I feel sorry for him. It's going to be a shock when he discovers his partner is such a rogue. I like Mr. Maynard."

Rather slowly and reluctantly Pat had returned to her side. His hands were itching to get at Mr. Jeen, and his dark face flushed again when he thought of what could have happened to Anne.

"He deserves hanging," he muttered between his teeth.

"I quite agree," said Mrs. Smythe. "Anne, you're not fit to be left alone –"

"She'll never be alone again," said Pat, and glanced at Anne's mother pointedly. "Mrs. Smythe, you look tired. May I suggest you go to bed? It's nearly three o'clock."

She gave a delighted chuckle in reply and patted her daughter's head gently as she passed the end of the settee.

"Don't keep her up too long," she advised as she reached the door. "Goodnight, dears."

"Goodnight," they said in unison, and in the silence that followed they heard her bedroom door close. Anne started playing with the flour bag and Pat, finding his hands were trembling a little, started to fill his pipe.

"Well?" she asked softly, raising her head at last. "Did you wish to speak to me or can I go to bed too?"

The glint of amusement came into his eyes and in a sudden

movement he put down his pipe and knelt down on the floor by her side.

"Anne, I'm sorry for the way I've behaved since I found out who you were," he said sincerely. "Do you think you can understand how I felt about it?"

"I'm sure I can," she answered. "Believe me, Pat, I've thought and worried over it for months. The last thing I ever wanted to do was to hurt you." Her fingers were tracing the little lines round his eyes and he caught her hand.

"This is the first time I've ever been on my knees to anyone. And I wouldn't be here now if I didn't love you. Listen, sweet. I hated Anne Carrington-Smythe, I love Anne Smith. Can you tell me which of them I have to ask to marry me? I'm rather confused."

"I should simply ask me," said Anne softly. "At the moment neither the Society girl nor the cook exist. The person you see sitting here is an extremely happy one because of what you've just said."

"Then you *will* marry me? As soon as the river goes down and we can go into town?"

She nodded through a mist of happy tears. "Yes, Pat."

He sighed deeply and pressed his lips against the hand he was still holding tightly in his own.

"I suppose I should have waited," he murmured. "Until Mr. Maynard has finished his inquisition —"

"Forget that," she interrupted him quickly. "After tonight, or rather, today, you're the new manager of Gum Valley, and I'll make it quite clear that it was no fault of yours."

"Thank you." He took the news very much for granted. "But John? If you're making me the manager, Anne, what about him? I can't turn the poor chap away from here."

"There's no need to, dear. He can stay at Gum Valley as long as he wishes. The only stipulation I make is that you don't take him with us when we go on our honeymoon."

Pat smiled. His love for Anne had proved stronger than his pride and he felt ridiculously pleased with himself. He had won her for himself alone, she had promised to marry him, and that proved Mr. Hall had no claim on her affections. He should never have doubted her, he thought, looking into her eyes. Anne would never play fast and loose with a man's affections.

"You don't mind me having so much money?" she asked sleepily from within the crook of his arm.

"I'll help you spend it," he promised.

"On what?"

"We'll need two new tractors," Pat lifted his head and gazed across the room. "A new header, a new electricity plant. There are many alterations necessary, things that should have been done years ago. Rusty is leaving, he announced the fact this evening, so we'll need a new groom as well as a new cook. After this you're not going back to the kitchen –"

"Why not? I've discovered that I like cooking."

"As my fiancée you're not cooking for the men any more. That's an order, Anne, do you understand?"

A faint rebelliousness showed on her face, he saw it and thrust out his jaw, quite prepared to argue about it if necessary. Anne relaxed.

"Yes, Pat," she said meekly.

"And now you're going to bed."

"Yes, Pat," she said again as he moved her from the settee and carried her across the room.

"I have an idea," he remarked thoughtfully, "that you won't always give way to me in such a meek manner."

"No," she agreed. "I shan't. Life without a few arguments to brighten things up wouldn't be worth living!"

They laughed softly together and because he was not looking where he was going he stumbled and bumped against Joy's bed in the half light from the uncurtained windows. The little girl sat bolt upright, her eyes round with fright.

"Oh!"

"It's only us," said her uncle quickly. "Anne has hurt her leg," he added in explanation. "That's why I'm carrying her to bed."

Joy shook back her hair and looked at them. Anne's arm was round her uncle's neck and her cheek was resting confidently against his. Her eyes widened.

"I think Joy ought to know," murmured Anne, watching the child's face. "She's been hoping this would happen."

"Has she indeed? Scamp, I'm going to marry Anne."

Joys lips parted in a smile of delight. She fumbled for words and the one that finally tumbled out made the other two smile with her.

"Scrumptious!"

The scene the following morning was precisely the same which had greeted them all the previous day. The river flowed strongly, still bringing with it large logs, trees and piles of debris, but it had not risen any more and hopes began to rise that it had started to drop in the higher reaches. The sun shone from a bright blue sky on to the waterlogged paddocks and there was a strange beauty in the sight of the gum trees standing with their shadows distorted by the rippling waters around them. One or two long-legged herons were standing majestically on a patch of mud and overhead the galahs and cockatoos wheeled in the still hot air.

When Mr. Jeen looked towards the river he shuddered. In the light of the morning the horror of the night was unbelievable. It was not difficult to imagine Anne's body floating away across the paddock which looked now like a deep gigantic lake, and swirling in the current of the main stream. He wondered how long it would be before, battered and bruised, it would catch in the branches of a tree and hang there until someone discovered it.

Perhaps not for so long; once it was known she was missing the jackaroo would start an extensive search around the homestead and for as far as it was possible beyond it. Mr. Jeen shuddered again. So far the household was behaving normally; perhaps everyone thought Anne was over in the kitchen preparing breakfast.

Pat Kennedy came on to the verandah and a curious look passed over his face at the sight of the solicitor. He nodded curtly and went in search of Roddie, who was gazing with distaste at the water still around his car.

"No sign of it dropping yet," he said gloomily. "I wish that radio was working."

"If there's been no more rain further back it will soon begin to go down." Pat lit his pipe and looked the other man in the eyes. "Mr. Hall, I want to tell you something." And in the quick sentences he explained what had happened while the homestead was asleep. Roddie's eyes grew round and he clenched his fists.

"Why, the dirty dog!" he exclaimed. "I'd like to get my hands on him!"

"That's my privilege," said Pat curtly. "But at Anne's request we must refrain. She has promised me, though, that she won't interfere with the law of justice. We can prove Jeen has been swindling her, to the tune of many thousands of pounds, and he'll have to stand his trial. Mr. Maynard has called a conference at nine-thirty and I want you to be there to keep an eye on that wily solicitor partner of his."

"With pleasure!" cried Roddie promptly.

"He might decide the river would be the lesser of two evils and I'm determined he's not going to take that way out. There's another thing," he added slowly, watching Roddie's face. "Anne and I are engaged."

Roddie did not flinch. Somehow he managed to smile and his grip on Pat's hand was hard and genuine.

"I'm glad. Congratulations. Hope you'll both be happy. She's a grand girl, I've known her since she was knee-high," he said shamelessly. "Been friends all our lives, you know. Like brother and sister."

Some of the wariness went from Pat's eyes at that piece of news. So that explained Roddie's welcome and his gentle familiarity. He smiled with great good humour and went in whistling for the breakfast Mrs. Smythe had prepared.

Prompt at nine-thirty Mr. Maynard returned to the dining-room with a sheaf of papers in his hands. Mr. Jeen followed him slowly. He could not understand why no one had mentioned Anne's absence; surely someone had missed her by now. He fidgeted about in his chair, darting anxious glances round the room, starting each time the door opened to admit someone. Pat watched him with a sardonic gleam in his eyes. By keeping Anne well out of the way and not even alluding to her he was producing the psychological effect he wanted. Roddie came in and sat on a chair near the door, Mrs. Smythe entered with the remark that this concerned her daughter, so naturally it concerned her, and finally Mr. Norton wandered in, looked at Pat enquiringly and sat down quietly on the chair indicated. He had no idea at all why he had been asked to come into this room, but Pat had told him to be there, so here he was.

No one spoke, they waited in perfect silence and still Anne did not make an appearance. Mr. Maynard cleared his throat once or twice and looked at each face with perplexity. His partner was seated on the edge of his chair, his hands gripped tightly together.

"Miss Carrington-Smythe —" began Mr. Maynard.

"I haven't seen her this morning," said Roddie from the door.

"Nor I," added Pat truthfully.

"She'll be coming," said Mrs. Smythe. "Supposing you make a start, Mr. Maynard."

"I can't, dear — Mrs. — er — Smythe. All this naturally concerns your daughter, as you stated when you came in here, it would be – er – useless to proceed without her."

"Anne wasn't in the kitchen this morning," stated Mr. Norton, looking at Pat. "Jan prepared breakfast."

"That's odd," Pat frowned, inwardly pleased at the innocent way John had made the remark.

"Very odd," cried Mrs. Smythe. "She didn't breakfast with us, either." Which was true; she had taken a tray into Anne's room.

There was another silence and Mr. Jeen became aware that three people were looking at him with accusation in their eyes. Mr. Maynard sensed something amiss and leaned back in his chair with a puzzled look on his face.

His partner could not stand the pregnant silence any longer. "Why are you all looking at me?" he asked, his voice rising a little.

"We were just wondering where Miss Smith could have gone to," said Pat. "Do you know?"

"Me? Of course not! Why should I?" There was panic in his face now.

"When did you last see her?" asked that quiet ruthless voice.

"Last night. In – in the sitting room."

"You're sure you didn't see her after that?"

"I went to bed," cried Mr. Jeen. He glanced at his partner, wanting confirmation of that fact.

Mr. Maynard had always been a truthful man. "You didn't come with me, Lionel," he said. "You said you wished to complete your task in the office."

"Er – yes. I'd forgotten that," mentally Mr. Jeen cursed the elder man's honesty.

"What were you doing in the office?" asked Mrs. Smythe with great interest. "You told me earlier in the evening that you'd finished in there."

"Just one or two things I needed." Mr. Jeen stood up. "And it's useless trying to talk round the main idea, Kennedy. We know you're responsible for the loss of all the money from Gum Valley."

"We're not concerned with money at present," said Pat coldly. "We were discussing Miss Smith."

"I haven't seen her," he cried wildly. "Why should I see her? What need was there for me to see her?"

"Why isn't she here now?"

"I don't know, I tell you. I went into the office for something and then returned. Mr. Maynard was asleep, he didn't hear me –"

"How did you manage to get your shoes and socks soaking wet?"

"My shoes?" Mr. Jeen's face went pale and he looked quickly at the man facing him. How much did he know, why was he playing with him like this? Had he already found Miss Carrington-Smythe's body? Even if he had it would tell him nothing.

"Yes, your shoes," snapped Pat. "If you don't know how you got them wet I'll tell you. You saw someone watching you through the window, and after you had turned out the lamp you went on to the verandah by way of the French windows. Then you hit the person who was sitting on the retainer wall –"

"Oh, my God!" Mr. Jeen sank back with his head between his hands, his body trembling violently. "How did you know?"

"After that you went on hitting her until she disappeared in the flood water. You ran to your room, forgetting this –" Pat withdrew the flour bag from behind him. "Which, together with the figures Miss Smith took the precaution of getting a day or two ago, is proof of what you've been doing during the past few years. With Miss Smith out of the way there would be no one who knew for certain it was you and not me who was robbing her and Gum Valley."

Mr. Jeen looked towards the door, met Roddie's icy glance

and sank back again in his chair. His partner was staring at him with horror in his eyes.

"Lionel! Are these accusations true?" he asked slowly.

"Yes," muttered Mr. Jeen in an almost inaudible voice.

"You robbed Miss Smythe and then –" the old solicitor's voice faded away in sheer disbelief.

"Pushed her off the wall," concluded Pat savagely.

"I didn't mean to do that," moaned the other, completely unnerved by now. "She confessed she was spying on me and I saw red. I didn't mean her to fall back like that."

"Yet you left her," shouted Pat, his face dark with rage. "You left her in the dark, in that muddy slimy water without calling for help." He started from his chair and Anne, who had been listening outside the door, thought it time she interfered. She hobbled into the room as Pat finally lost his temper and flung himself at the cowed man before him.

"You promised me," she cried, dragging at his arms. "Darling, you promised you wouldn't touch him. Sit down again," she added gently. "Mr. Maynard knows the truth now and I don't think there's much need for more discussion. I'm sorry it's all happened like this," she turned to the old solicitor, "but I wanted to prove beyond all doubt that Pat was not responsible for the thefts. He did alter the accounts, he was quite frank about it, but every penny was used only for the station. The men knew what was happening and they're all prepared to swear to that effect."

Mr. Maynard nodded with comprehension. "I understand. It was my partner who robbed you over the years. He read the letters when they first arrived, it was easy – Yes, I understand," he said heavily. "He always insisted upon working Gum Valley's accounts. When you first came to me and told me you wished to come here I had to confess I knew little about it."

"I'm sorry, Mr. Maynard," said Anne again. "It's been a great shock to you," he nodded slowly, "but to expose Mr. Jeen was the only thing that mattered to me. Pat's name had to be cleared. I'll overlook," she glanced coldly at the beaten Mr. Jeen, "your attack on me last night, although both my mother and Pat say I'm a fool."

"You are," agreed Roddie from the door. "He should be made to suffer for what he made you suffer."

Anne shook her head. "No. I'll leave Mr. Maynard with the unpleasant task of sorting out my accounts and prosecuting his partner. That will be enough. You see," she smiled happily at Mr. Maynard, "Pat and I are going to be married, and I don't want any publicity and court appearances to spoil the beginning of our mrried life."

"You won't be returning to Sydney?"

"Not for a long time. We've a lot to do here. We need new tractors, a new header –"

Despite the seriousness of the moment and the look on Mr. Jeen's face, Pat burst out laughing, and to complete his happiness there came a sudden shout from outside, and Joy and Dick, hand in hand, came splashing through the water towards the house.

"It's started to drop," cried Dick excitedly. "The marker I put in last night is clear, it's gone down over an inch!"

All but Mr. Jeen moved towards the window. He continued to sit with his head in his hands, utterly beaten. The news that the river was dropping brought no relief. Once the roads were clear he would have to return and face whatever was coming to him.

Pat was standing with his arm round Anne's shoulders. Dick's news made her heart leap; once the roads were clear she and Pat would be able to get into Murra Creek and break the good news of their engagement to his parents and after that there would be a quiet ceremony in the creeper-covered church which stood in the shade of the giant kurrajongs, and they would return from there to the peace of Gum Valley. She lifted her head to smile at Pat, but he was gazing over the distant paddocks, busy with a vision of his own. He was thinking of walking in the sunshine towards a river which flowed gently between its banks again, with this girl by his side and with his son perched on his shoulder.

Mills & Boon's Paperbacks

MARCH

THE BLACK EAGLE BY ANNE HAMPSON

Because she resembled his long-dead fiancée Roxanne was carried off by the mysterious Mexican Don Juan Armando Ramirez. In time, Roxanne's hatred of her husband turned to love . . . but what chance had she of reaching his heart?

CASTLES IN SPAIN BY REBECCA STRATTON

Holly was delighted to have the chance of visiting the Spanish castle where her aunt had lived since her marriage. Don José Delgaro gave her a charming welcome, but it was his son Marcos whose attitude really puzzled Holly. Was he trifling with her until he married the attractive Helena Mendez?

THE MAN AT KAMBALA BY KAY THORPE

Sara lived with her father at Kambala and was accustomed to doing as she pleased there. She certainly didn't reckon much of the ideas of Steve York, the impossible man who came to take charge in her father's absence. "It's asking for trouble to run round a game reserve as if it were a play park," he told her. Was Sara right to ignore him?

THE SILVER STALLION BY IRIS DANBURY

Lucie Durrant went to the Canary Islands on a working holiday looking for new ideas for the jewellery that she designed. Her call on the attractive Joel Barron was of a purely business nature, but later, as she came to know him better, she began to wonder if that was all he meant to her . . .

THE GLASS CASTLE BY VIOLET WINSPEAR

"Out in the East they say that the mind of a woman is a jungle, and it is the one jungle in which a man should never get lost." That was the code by which Edwin Trequair lived – or so he told Heron. Why then did he ask her to marry him? Could Heron ever understand such a strange, arrogant man?

20p net each

Mills & Boon's Paperbacks

MARCH (contd.)

THE MAN AT LA VALAISE BY MARY WIBBERLEY

Sacha Donnelly decided to holiday in Provence on her own and certainly didn't bargain on having to share her cottage with three strange men. How she longed to escape from Nikolai, dark and dangerous, who had forced her to remain there. But soon Sacha was to wonder if she really wanted to get away ...

THE TREE OF IDLENESS BY ELIZABETH HUNTER

When Caroline went to visit her aunt in Cyprus she looked forward to renewing her acquaintance with the country and the people. But how was she to deal with Philip Klearchos, dark and disturbing, who warned her, "I may take your education in hand and give you a taste of what being a woman can mean ..."

A SENSE OF BELONGING BY LILIAN PEAKE

When Carina fell in love with Marcus de Verrier, the man who was grooming her voice for stardom, his reaction was predictable. "Many students fall in love with their teachers. It's nothing unusual. An occupational hazard, in fact. But I prefer to call it infatuation, which will pass with time." How could she make him realise that this just wasn't true?

SHADE OF THE PALMS BY ROBERTA LEIGH

To Stephen Brandon, Julia was no more than Miss Watson, his unflappable, highly efficient secretary. A dowdy woman wearing unfashionable clothes, sensible shoes and spectacles, he would have thought if he'd considered the matter at all. But he was to discover that appearances can be deceptive and that there was a totally unexpected side to Julia.

PEPPERTREE LANE BY LINDEN GRIERSON

Jean Delaney was very grateful to her Uncle Gerald, who had given her and her mother and young brother a home – but Gerald's foster-son Rob was convinced that the whole affair was a confidence trick and that the whole family were out to make what they could from the old man. Was he right to be suspicious?

20p net each

FREE!

YOUR COPY OF OUR MAGAZINE OF
MILLS & BOON ROMANCES NOW AVAILABLE

If you enjoyed reading this MILLS & BOON romance and would like a list of other MILLS & BOON romances available, you can receive a free magazine by completing the coupon below and posting it off today. This opportunity to read more about MILLS & BOON romances should not be missed. Your free magazine will be posted off to you immediately.

Over the page are listed 50 selections from our current catalogue. Why not contact your local stockist to obtain these books? However, should you have any difficulty please write to us at MILLS & BOON READER SERVICE, P.O. BOX 236, 14 Sanderstead Road, S. Croydon, Surrey, CR2 oYG, England, ticking the titles you require, and enclosing your remittance. All Mills & Boon paperbacks ordered through the Reader Service are 20p. Please note to cover postage and handling, will United Kingdom readers add 2p per book. Overseas readers are asked to add 1op per book and use International Money Orders where possible.

Please send me the free Mills & Boon Romance magazine ☐

Please send me the titles ticked ☐

I enclose £... (No C.O.D.)

Name .... Miss/Mrs.

Address ....

Town/City ....

County/Country........................... Postal/Zip Code...........

MB2/74

HAVE YOU MISSED ANY OF THESE MILLS & BOON ROMANCES?

ALL PRICED AT 20p   SEE OVER FOR HANDY ORDER FORM   PLEASE TICK YOUR REQUIREMENTS